BI   JM

AST

ROTHERHAM LIBRARY & INFORMATION SERVICE

This book must be returned by the date specified at the time of issue as
the DATE DUE FOR RETURN.
The loan may be extended (personally, by post, telephone or online) for
a further period if the book is not required by another reader, by quoting
the above number / author / title.

Enquiries: 01709 336774

www.rotherha~   k/libraries

Alison Roberts is a New Zealander, currently lucky enough to be living in the South of France. She is also lucky enough to write for the Mills & Boon Medical Romance line. A primary school teacher in a former life, she is now a qualified paramedic. She loves to travel and dance, drink champagne, and spend time with her daughter and her friends.

Also by Alison Roberts

Sleigh Ride with the Single Dad

Rescued Hearts miniseries

The Doctor's Wife for Keeps
Twin Surprise for the Italian Doc

Bondi Bay Heroes collection

The Shy Nurse's Rebel Doc
Finding His Wife, Finding a Son
by Marion Lennox
Healed by Her Army Doc
by Meredith Webber
Rescued by Her Mr Right

Discover more at millsandboon.co.uk.

RESCUED BY HER MR RIGHT

ALISON ROBERTS

MILLS & BOON

For Linda and Meredith,
with much love.

CHAPTER ONE

SHE HAD BEEN aware of the sound for longer than she'd realised.

It wasn't until Harriet Collins had finally reached the flat part of this cliff walk that her focus relaxed enough to acknowledge the sound.

A dog barking.

It had just been part of the background for what felt like a long time. A background that included the warmth of a late Australian spring day and the sound of waves rolling onto the rocky shore far below where she was now. Her concentration had been on more important things. Like the occasional uneven steps and rough stony patches on this clifftop walkway.

Like the pain in her leg that had reached an intolerable level a while back but hadn't been allowed to do more than slow her down because Harriet needed to find out how far she could push it before it let her down completely and refused to keep her upright—as it had so many times over the long, long months of her rehabilitation so far.

Someone else must be walking this track, she decided, as she paused long enough to fish her water bottle from the mesh side pouch of her small backpack. She could feel other lumpy shapes inside the pack as she slotted the bottle back into place.

Exciting lumps. She had chosen this walk to try out her new camera for the first time. And that expensive zoom lens. When she found the right spot, she could wait until the sun was starting to set and hopefully capture some amazing shots of the waves crashing on those fearsome rocks at shore level. She had a headlamp tucked inside as well, which should make it safe enough for her to get back down the track to where she'd parked her car when daylight was fading.

It did seem odd, though, that this dog was being so vocal. And the sound wasn't getting any fainter, which you would expect if an overexcited pet was running ahead of its person on a long walk. If anything, it was getting louder, as Harriet started walking again.

Her limp was more pronounced than it had been for some time but that was only to be expected after that long uphill stretch. The paracetamol she had swallowed along with that drink of water should kick in soon and, by the time she'd had a good rest while she took her photographs, she should be ready to tackle the return trip.

The barking got louder and Harriet stopped in her tracks when she saw the dark shape rushing towards her.

A beat of fear stopped her inward breath.

A dog attack? *Really?* After so many months of fighting to get her life approaching anything like normal, was she about to get sent back to square one by being mauled by a big dog? To be even more disfigured than she was already?

No way…

The sound that Harriet let out was a half-scream merged with an angry growl that expressed quite a lot about the struggle she'd been through and her desperation to not allow any new setbacks.

It seemed to work. The dog stopped in its tracks, too. And it stopped barking. It stared at Harriet.

Harriet stared back.

It was a black Labrador but not nearly as fat as most Labs she'd met. Maybe it got a lot of exercise running along these clifftop tracks with its owner.

Where was its owner? When he or she appeared, Harriet might have something to say about letting their dog run loose and frighten people. What if she'd had children with her?

The dog started barking again. It turned, ran a few steps and then stopped to look back at her. This time the barking felt like an attempt to communicate something.

'Oh, for heaven's sake,' Harriet muttered aloud. 'You've seen too many Lassie movies.'

But it felt right to follow the dog. Cautiously, because it was taking her off this well-marked and relatively flat pathway. Through long grass and big boulders towards the edge of the cliff. The dog didn't stop until it seemed to be standing on the very edge. It peered down the cliff and then turned back to Harriet. Its barking sounded more urgent now.

One step and then another brought Harriet nearer the dog.

'What is it?' she asked. 'What's wrong?'

A tail wagged encouragement and the dog sat down as Harriet got within touching distance. It nudged her hand and licked her.

'At least you're friendly,' she said. 'What's your name?'

There was a collar with a disc on it. 'Harry? Are you kidding me? That's *my* name.'

Harry the dog nudged her again and then stood up to peer over the edge again.

'Okay...' Harriet lay down, just to be safe, and inched forward.

It wasn't a straight drop but it was steep enough to be dangerous with areas of loose scree amongst boulders and weathered shrubs that were clinging to life. At the point where the intermittent vegetation gave up, there was a drop onto a ledge. She couldn't see the whole ledge but what she could see made a shiver run down her spine.

Legs.

And one of them was twisted at a very unnatural angle.

'Hey...' she yelled. 'Can you hear me? Are you conscious?'

There was no answering call. No flicker of movement from the legs.

'It's okay,' Harriet yelled again. 'I'm going to call for help.'

She hauled her mobile phone out of the pocket of her cargo pants and then punched in the emergency three-digit number, giving a curt response of 'Ambulance' when she was asked what service she required.

'I'm at the top of the Kookaburra walkway,' she told the call taker in the communications centre. 'There's someone who's fallen from the cliff. He's on a ledge about a hundred metres from the top and...and he's not responding to calls. I can see from here that he's probably got a badly fractured leg.'

'No...' she said a minute later. 'There's no access from the top unless it's by abseiling. I think we're going to need a helicopter.' She listened for a few seconds and then interrupted the young woman she was speaking to.

'Look...my name is Harriet Collins. I'm an intensive care nurse at Bondi Bayside Hospital but I'm also a member of the Specialist Disaster Response team based there.'

It wasn't exactly true. Not now... But they hadn't yet officially removed her from the membership list, had they?

'I know what I'm talking about, okay? We need a helicopter. This is a winch job. Anything else is going to take too long.'

And that was that. Help was on its way and there was nothing more that Harriet could do other than sit and wait and maybe signal the helicopter crew when they got close.

Harry the dog didn't think so. He nudged her elbow and his whine was an easily interpreted plea.

Harriet peered over the edge of the cliff again.

The dog walker had trainers on his feet. And socks. And…yes…the foot on the leg that looked normal was moving.

'Hey…' Harriet could hear the alarm bell going off in her head. She yelled even louder this time. 'Don't move, okay? You're safe where you are and help's coming. But…just don't *move*…'

If he'd been unconscious, he might have a head injury and not be thinking clearly. What if he managed to drag himself right off that ledge? There'd be no chance of survival if he finished the drop to where the surf was roiling around those black, jagged rocks.

Had she been wrong in saying that ledge was a hundred metres from the top of the cliff? It looked more like fifty at second guess. And maybe it wouldn't have needed abseilers to get down. There were enough protruding rocks to provide good footholds and those scrappy little trees would give handholds for balance if you didn't trust them with your whole body weight.

It didn't need another nudge from Harry the dog to trigger Harriet's decision. It didn't seem to need any conscious thought at all. If she had stopped to think, she would have known how crazy this was. That her bad leg couldn't possibly cope with this challenge.

But Harriet didn't think. She just sat on her bottom, holding a branch of the nearest shrunken tree and let herself slide, very slowly, until her feet reached the first rock below her. The foot of her bad leg touched it first and a spear of pain lanced upwards to reach her thigh but her leg didn't crumple and, as soon as she transferred to her weight to her good foot, the pain receded.

When she did it again, she made sure it was her strong leg that found a solid object first. Now she was several metres below where Harry had started running back and forth on the flat area, barking encouragement, and the enormity of what she'd started was enough to make her head spin for a moment or two.

At least this incarnation of Lassie was someone to talk to.

'I'm not sure that this was such a good idea,' she told him. 'I'm going to have to crawl sideways to reach that next tree. Do you reckon it's got strong roots?'

Harry the dog seemed to think so.

She had to cling to the next rock for a minute, to get over the fright of her foot slipping a little in the scree. She didn't look down. Instead, she looked up at the black head that was getting smaller every time she looked.

'What you don't know,' she said casually, 'is that until very recently I was wearing a pretty hard-core brace on my leg. Because I had a rock that landed on it a while back and it was so squashed they almost had to chop it off. Yeah… I know dogs can manage quite well without one of their legs but it's a bit more of a problem for a person.'

The sound of the waves was getting louder and Harriet knew perfectly well that the dog couldn't hear what she was saying and wouldn't understand if he could but it seemed to be helping her.

'But look at me right now… It almost feels like I'm back in the SDR team and I don't mind telling you that that's the thing I miss the most about my old life.'

Except that if this was a team callout, she'd be appropriately dressed in heavy-duty overalls and with a hard hat and gloves for more protection. And she'd be on the end of a rope with people who knew what they were doing holding the other end to prevent a fall that would have meant two victims instead of only one.

If she'd done anything this irresponsible as a team member, their leader, Blake Cooper, would have probably sacked her, and Kate and Sam would have been watching her with horror. But she wasn't a team member any more and she never could be, with the disability that was highly likely to be permanent now. A weak leg. Pain levels that could be hard to manage. A mindset that was very different from the passionate and adventurous person she'd been all those months ago.

Maybe she was going to get stuck herself and the rescue crew would have to winch two people off this cliff and she'd cop an awful lot of flak. But…

But the fact that she was even trying to do this—that she *wanted* to do this so much—made her feel like the real Harriet Collins had finally stepped out from the black mist she'd been shrouded in for so long.

And she was more than halfway down now. That ledge was starting to look bigger and hiding the terrifying drop below it. Another controlled slide on her bottom, a careful climb over a tumble of rocks without trusting her weight to her bad leg and then a downward, sideways crawl and she could almost stand up to push her way past rough bunches of tussock and through the stunted trees onto the ledge.

Harry's owner was probably in his sixties, his grey hair matted with a stain of blood and a badly bruised and grazed arm. And he was groaning.

'Hey…' Harriet crouched beside him, picking up his hand and then feeling for his pulse. 'My name's Harry. Same as your dog…'

The man's eyes opened. 'Harry…'

'He's fine. He's up on top of the cliff. He came to find me and get help for you. Just like Lassie.'

The man's eyes closed but his lips twisted into a smile. 'Not so much. It was Harry who went over the edge. Got…stuck on a rock and I went down to help. I lost my footing and…argh…that *really* hurts…'

'Your leg? Or is it something else?'

'My leg…and…and my head doesn't feel great.'

'What's your name?'

'Eddie. Eddie Denton.'

'Okay, Eddie. Take a deep breath for me. Does that hurt?'

'No. Feels okay…'

'That's great. We don't need to worry about your breathing then. And you've got a good pulse so that means your blood pressure's still okay.'

'You a doctor, Harry?'

'No, I'm a nurse. I worked in the Intensive Care Unit at Bondi Bayside, although I'm somewhere else at the moment. But I'm also a member of a specialist rescue team there.'

She was checking Eddie out as she kept talking. 'I'm just going to have a feel of your tummy, okay? Does that hurt?'

'No. It's just my leg.'

The pain from an obvious femoral fracture could well be masking something happening internally but there was nothing Harriet could do other than keep Eddie company and make sure he didn't move and fall further. There was no time to do anything else, anyway. She could see the dot of the approaching helicopter now and only seconds later the sound of the rotors drowned out the faint barking she could still hear from the top of the cliff.

This was one of the bright red and yellow helicopters of the ambulance service here in Sydney and the crew member she could see leaning out from the skid and preparing to be winched down would be one of the elite, intensive care paramedics that dealt with calls like this. It was a relief to see the big pack of gear being attached to the winch line along with a stretcher but she expected nothing less from a team who were well used to dealing with emergencies on the shorelines of this huge coastal city.

What she would never have expected was to be addressed as if this paramedic knew her.

'Harry? How did you end up on this ledge?' He pushed up the visor of his helmet as he unhooked the gear and then held the winch line clear, giving the winch operator the 'thumbs up' sign to retrieve the hook. 'I thought the job had been called in from up at the track.'

'Oh, my God…' Harriet's jaw dropped. 'When did you start working on the choppers, Jack?'

'Months ago.' His tone was clipped. Cold, even? 'Fill me in, Harry.'

'This is Eddie Denton. He's sixty-three. He slipped and fell after trying to get his dog out of trouble.'

There was a nagging voice at the back of her head telling her that she deserved the brush-off. How many times had she done that to Jack after the accident, when he'd tried to visit her?

But not being part of the team any more had made it too painful to be reminded of how devastating the loss of this part of her life had been. And he'd given up eventually, just the way everybody else had stopped talking about it. Harriet couldn't actually remember the last time she'd heard Jack's name mentioned.

'Hiya, Eddie. I'm Jack Evans. I've come

to get you out of here, mate. How are you feeling?'

'Gotta sore leg.'

'Fractured mid-shaft femur,' Harriet put in. 'Limb baselines are intact.'

'Anything else I should know about?'

'Head injury. I'm pretty sure he was unconscious when I arrived on scene and he's been complaining about a headache.'

'And that arm?'

'I don't think it's fractured but it's badly bruised and there's a fair bit of skin missing. Blood loss was minimal as far as I can tell.'

It could have been worse. If Eddie had been bleeding badly, she could have stopped that. Did that justify her putting herself in so much danger and giving the rescue crew another person to manage? She hadn't really thought about the consequences when she'd started that climb down, had she?

Instinct had overridden sense.

Or maybe it was because she hadn't been able to resist the pull of being that person again. The one that did the dangerous stuff because she could potentially save a life.

'Can you find some dressings in that pack? I'd like to get an IV in and some pain relief on board before we get a traction splint on that leg.'

It wasn't just Eddie who had a sore leg. The jolt of pain as Harriet moved to open Jack's pack was almost enough to make her stumble. Maybe it was a good thing that they were on a relatively narrow ledge above a dangerous drop so it was a perfectly normal thing to do to crawl carefully from one point to another.

Jack wouldn't have even noticed.

'You okay, Harry?'

The swift glance from those dark eyes and the furrow between them told Harriet that he'd noticed her wincing, all right. She broke the eye contact abruptly. She didn't want anybody's pity but to be pitied by Jack was worse, somehow. He was one of the younger members of the SDR team and one of the best. He was going places, young Jack Evans, but he wasn't cocky about it. He was, in fact, one of the nicest people Harriet had ever known.

In her old life…

'Be careful,' was all Jack added. 'We're a long way up. Hand me that IV roll, would you?'

She handed over the roll that contained everything Jack needed to insert an IV. The wipes, cannulas, Luer plugs, flushes and adhesive covers. She didn't need reminding of how far above sea level they were. Every few seconds, even given the sound of the helicopter hovering nearby, she could hear the rolling crash of a huge wave below.

'Sharp scratch, Eddie. There you go… Are you allergic to anything that you know of?'

'Nah…not that I know of.'

Harriet had all the sterile dressings and a bandage in her hands so that she could cover the raw wounds on Eddie's arm but she stayed by the pack for a moment longer. Jack was going to need a giving set and a bag of saline to set up fluids that would keep Eddie's vein open in case he needed more intravenous drugs. The morphine would definitely be helping his pain level within the next few minutes.

'What score would you give your pain now, Eddie? Out of ten, like before?'

'I reckon it's only a five now. Maybe even a four.'

'Good man. We're going to get that splint on your leg in a tick. And then I'm going to get you up into our nice comfy chopper.'

'But what about Harry?'

'We'll take her, too, don't you worry. I'm not about to let her try climbing up this cliff by herself. God knows how she managed to get down to you in the first place.' Jack was waiting for Harriet to look up as she snagged the bandage she'd wound around Eddie's arm with a crocodile clip to keep it secure. 'Good job,' he added as he finally caught her gaze.

He sounded impressed. And not the least bit cold. Quite the opposite, in fact.

'No.' Eddie shook his head. 'I meant Harry—my dog...'

'Oh…right…'

'He's a hero,' Harriet said. 'I wouldn't have found Eddie if it hadn't been for Harry. He came and got me and made me follow him.'

Jack grinned. 'Like Lassie, huh?'

Harriet found herself smiling back. 'Just like Lassie.'

The shared smile broke whatever odd tension she had been aware of ever since Jack had touched down on this ledge. It was a link back to the very real friendship they'd shared during their time together with the SDR team. A friendship that Harriet couldn't deny she'd shunned since her accident because it was such an integral aspect of the part of the life she'd lost for ever.

But maybe there was a way back? To a small part of what she'd lost, anyway.

And that felt good.

'In that case, I'll call the crew.' Jack nodded, reaching for his radio. 'We'll get someone to head up the track and find him. Don't you worry, Eddie. He'll be well

looked after until we can get him home
for you.'

Whether it was the relief of knowing his
pet would be rescued, or the effects of the
narcotic pain relief, Eddie seemed to relax
into the care they were giving him. It was
painful to get the traction splint locked into
place and doing its job but, for this kind
of fracture, it was essential to get control
of any internal bleeding and added pain
of the movement that would be happening very soon.

'I'll take Eddie up on the stretcher and
then I'll come back down for you and the
pack.' Jack raised his arm to signal the
crew in the hovering helicopter that he
was ready for the winch line to be lowered again. 'Okay?'

Harriet nodded.

For several long minutes, she was alone
on the ledge, watching Jack control the
swinging of the stretcher Eddie was
strapped onto as it was lifted skywards.
And then she saw it being tipped and
dragged into the cabin of the helicopter.

It seemed to take a long time until Jack was standing on the skid again, ready for his second descent, but she watched him coming down with an increasing sense of relief.

There was no way she could have climbed back up that cliff.

It was no wonder that Jack had been impressed that she'd managed it at all. The last time he'd seen her, her leg had been skewered with long pins and encased in the rods of external fixation for a fracture that had been bad enough for her to have had to give consent to amputation if that had been deemed the best option during her surgery.

He'd been so determinedly cheerful, she remembered. He'd brought a brand of chocolate she'd once announced was her all-time favourite and some magazines, but the choice had been unfortunate, including the latest edition of an emergency medicine journal. And, okay, maybe that publication had also previously been favourite reading material but it had been the last thing she'd wanted to see then.

The visit had been awkward. What did they have in common other than the team callouts, training sessions and rare social occasions? Jack was a good six years younger than Harriet. Just a mate.

At least he hadn't been around to see her limping return to work at Bondi Bayside. If he was with the helicopter crew he wouldn't even be spending time in the emergency department, although he might still make an occasional visit to the intensive care unit if he wanted to follow up on a patient. Not that Harriet was working there any more—not when that environment needed people who could be quick on their feet when needed and in no danger from being distracted by pain or fatigue.

An echo of the awkwardness that had only increased between them until Jack didn't come to visit her any more reared its head as he arrived back on the ledge and helped Harriet into the 'nappy' harness that would hold her close to his body as they were winched back into the helicopter. Maybe it was a good thing that it was noisy and scary and there was no need to say anything other than to confirm she understood all the instructions.

The scariest part was when her feet lost contact with the relative safety of that ledge and she was dangling in mid-air, with the rocks of the cliff looking alarmingly close and the roiling surf a terrifying drop below.

Oddly, she felt safe at the same time.

Jack was big. Tall and muscly. Not with the kind of muscles that her ex-boyfriend Pete had nurtured in his gym sessions, though. Just like his looks were a complete contrast to the sun-streaked, surfer vibe that had attracted her to Pete in the first place. It felt like Jack had just been born that way, and maybe he had. The young paramedic had island heritage—Maori or Samoan—with the dark eyes and black hair that went with his olive skin. He had the gentleness that could come as such a pleasant surprise in a big man but he also had strength and that was what Harriet could feel surrounding her now as they rose slowly in this vast sky.

How long had it been since she'd felt a man's arms around her like this? Making her feeling safe. Cherished, almost.

Maybe that foolhardy challenge of climbing down that cliff had been worth it.

Just for this...

CHAPTER TWO

FUNNY HOW MANY thoughts could flash through your brain when you were dangling in mid-air. Even when most of your concentration was so focused on keeping both yourself and the person you were holding safe.

But the thoughts were there. Drifting past like fragments of a half-forgotten dream.

Because he *had* dreamed of this. Once upon a time.

Holding Harriet Collins in his arms…

Part of his soul had recognised her as the perfect woman the first time he'd met her, back when they had both been new and on their very first training session for the SDR team. Everything about her had been fascinating. Those shiny, auburn curls that bounced when she moved her head. The cute freckles that dusted her milky skin. Hazel eyes with the sparkle of sheer *joie de vivre*. That easy smile and the contagious gurgle of her laughter. How *nice* she was. Warm and open and friendly.

It had taken a long time to screw up the courage to ask her out on a date. He'd had to fight the doubts about how unlikely it was that she could be as interested in *him*. She was years older than he was. Older and wiser and with a circle of friends that were part of a very different world but the attraction was so strong, he'd had to try.

The sheer delight that she seemed to think it was a great idea had been short-lived. She'd seen it as no more than a mate suggesting a team outing, in fact, because she'd shared the invitation with those around them, including the new guy who'd just joined the team—a good-looking firie by the name of Pete Thompson.

And it had been that very night—that had been supposed to be his first date with Harriet—that the spark had been ignited between her and Pete. Jack had felt every jolt of electricity that had passed between them and every one of them had been tipped with the flame of rejection. Of not being good enough. Of not having the kind of charisma that blokes like Pete Thompson had. He knew that that charisma often came with a price. That they were often shallow, egotistical people.

But there'd been nothing that he could do, other than watch it happen. And accelerate. And he'd got over it. So Harriet wasn't for him? It didn't matter. They were still friends and he'd find someone else who made him feel this way—without those doubts that he'd made the mistake of ignoring. One of these days, he *would* experience that 'falling in love' business. Preferably with someone that he knew he would want to spend the rest of his life with.

Someone like Harriet Collins maybe, but with some island blood so that she could embrace being part of an extended family that could sometimes smother you with the responsibilities of belonging but would never tolerate being shut out of any dark times in your life.

The way Harriet had shut *him* out.

It still hurt, Jack realised, as they got close enough to where his crewmate, Matt, was leaning out of the chopper door, ready to pull Harriet to safety and unclip the nappy harness. It was almost a relief when he couldn't feel the shape of her body against his any longer.

He'd wanted to hold her in his arms so much, that day, when he'd gone to see her after the accident, still reeling from the shock of witnessing that rockfall on their team day out in the Blue Mountains with a day of abseiling training underway. He'd seen that rock hit Harriet and the fear that she'd been killed had made it seem like the ground had been opening up beneath him. A world without Harriet Collins could never be quite the same. He'd had to swipe tears of relief from his face when he'd heard that she'd come through the surgery and still had her leg but he'd known the moment he'd walked into her room for that first visit that even getting close enough to touch her wasn't going to be welcomed.

She'd put up a barrier that might have been transparent but it was impenetrable. And, from what Jack had heard over the last months, he hadn't been the only person who'd been relegated to the other side of that barrier. Harriet's life had fallen apart after the accident but it had been deemed none of his business, however much he might have wanted to try and help.

But she had needed his help today.

Welcomed it, in fact.

And it almost felt like that barrier had somehow evaporated—on her side, anyway. Perhaps he'd put up one of his own, to protect himself from having his friendship rejected again. From the reminders of that even more painful rejection of something that he'd believed could have been a whole lot more than simply friendship.

She was watching him now, as he and Matt made sure that Eddie was as comfortable as possible, monitored his vital signs and tried to check him out for any significant injuries that might have been missed. It was only a short flight to the nearest hospital so it was a busy time but Jack's glance caught Harriet's on more than one occasion—like when he'd tightened the loop anchoring the nasal cannula for oxygen and moved to attach the end of the tubing to the on-board supply. And when he reached up to change the flow rate on the IV fluids they were administering to stabilise Eddie's blood pressure.

What was so different about her?

She was a bit thinner, which was hardly surprising given the physical ordeal she'd been through. Her skin was paler. Because she wasn't outside every free moment she could find—doing fun runs or surfing or something? Her freckles had faded too but the change he was trying to identify wasn't anything negative. Quite the contrary. It was…a bit of a spark, that's what it was. As if a glimmer of the woman he'd admired so much had returned. A woman who'd all but vanished within weeks of that terrible accident.

The last time Jack had gone to visit her in hospital, she'd been fighting an infection that had again raised the awful possibility that her lower leg might have to be amputated. She had been feeling very unwell, lying there with intravenous antibiotics dripping into her arm, and the visit had been more than awkward. Jack had felt helpless and hated it.

Harriet had looked…hopeless, which had been even worse.

She hadn't wanted to see him. She certainly hadn't wanted to talk about the SDR, which was pretty much the only thing they had in common. And when she'd looked directly at him—just before she'd said it might be better if he left—her eyes had been like nothing he would have ever associated with Harriet. So dark. So flat you wouldn't know there were little golden flecks in that hazel warmth.

That was it in a nutshell. The sparkle was back. Not the way it had been but it

was there in the interest she was show-
ing in the information being recorded on
the ECG monitor and the new set of limb
baselines Matt was doing to check on the
blood supply to Eddie's leg below the level
of the fracture.

It had been there, as part of that smile,
when he'd made that lame joke about
Lassie.

As they came in to land at one of Sydney's larger hospitals, a long way from
Bondi Bayside, Jack leaned close and
raised his voice.

'Stay on board when we land. I'm off
duty once we get back to base and I can
take you home.'

'I left my car,' Harriet told him. 'Back
at the cliffs.'

'No worries. We'll sort it. We can check
that Lassie's been rescued, too.'

Her eyes widened as if she was surprised
he was worried about his patient's pet but
then her face softened as if she was re-
membering that it wasn't out of character

at all. It was the kind of person he'd always been.

Her smile—and her nod—told him that she liked that.

'Sounds great.' Harriet leaned close to Eddie as they were unhooking the stretcher ready to wheel him towards the waiting staff members on the far side of the helipad. 'I'll come and see you as soon as I can. Don't worry. I'll make sure Harry's okay.'

She would, too, Jack thought as he bent to move under the still moving rotors of the helicopter that would take them back to base very soon. She was that kind of person as well.

And he'd always loved that about her.

It felt like the old days.

The time when life had been full of excitement and promise. Before it had all come crashing down around her in such spectacular fashion.

The climb down that cliff face. Treating someone with traumatic injuries. Being winched into a helicopter and then flying over the city she loved so much. Somehow, in recent months she'd forgotten how gorgeous it was.

Being with Jack was another link to her past life and, oddly, she didn't have a compelling urge to push it away in order not to add weight to the miserable shroud of what she'd lost. Today, it didn't feel quite so lost and the reminder of what it had been like was poignant but also precious.

Jack's car was parked at the back of the air rescue base, far enough away from where they'd landed to make Harriet very aware of how far she'd pushed her new boundaries today.

'You okay?' Jack's sideways glance was casual. 'You could wait here while I get the car.'

Harriet didn't meet his gaze. 'I'm good. This is what I do now, Jack. I limp.'

The silence made her realise that she'd slipped back into that defensive mode that made her tone too sharp and pushed people away.

'Sorry,' she muttered. 'But I think I can make it. I need to try.'

'I'm sure you can make it. You climbed down a cliff today, didn't you? And you don't need to apologise. I understand…'

People said that a lot, with the best intentions, but it was never true, was it? You couldn't really understand unless it had happened to *you*.

But it felt like maybe Jack did understand. More than others, anyway.

'It will get better,' she told him. 'It's just that I've only been out of my brace for a week or so. And I probably did more today than I should have, even before I climbed down the cliff.'

'What *were* you doing up there? Testing yourself? Might be a good idea not to do stuff like that by yourself, you know.' His smile was crooked. 'Just sayin'…'

'Yeah, yeah… It was a bit of a test, I guess, but the real reason was to try out my new zoom lens. I wanted some shots of surf crashing on rocks, preferably as it got close to sunset when the light gets awesome.'

'You've really got into photography, haven't you? I saw you taking all the photos at Kate and Angus's wedding.'

She'd noticed him there as well. Not that she'd made any attempt to go and talk to him. She'd stayed behind that camera the whole time and had left as early as she could without being rude. It had been hard, being there but not being one of the team any longer.

'I really have.' It was a relief to reach the car and take the weight off her leg. A quick glance at her watch told Harriet that she could take some more painkillers soon. As soon as Jack wasn't around to notice because those sharp of eyes of his didn't miss much. Had he been aware that she'd avoided talking to him at the wedding?

'It started because I was taking photos of my leg, actually,' she found herself saying quietly as the car pulled out onto the road. 'I wanted a record so that, on bad days, I could remind myself that things were improving. And then I started taking photos of other stuff and I got hooked. Not only did I have a topic of conversation that had nothing to do with my leg but I could kind of hide behind the camera when I was out with other people. Win-win.'

She'd never admitted that to anyone. She'd kept people at a distance by being distant herself with a forced cheerfulness or, shamefully more often, a bad-tempered snappiness. Jack hadn't seen the worst of it but she knew she'd hurt him by reject-ing his support early on. Opening up, just a little, was a kind of peace offering and, judging by the intensity of the swift glance he gave her, he realised that it was a big thing.

'I'm sorry,' he said softly. 'I can only imagine how rough it's been for you.'

'Actually, I think it's me that should be apologising.'

'What on earth for?'

'I was horrible to you. When you came to visit. You didn't deserve that.'

Jack shrugged. He seemed to be concentrating on the road ahead. 'It was no big deal. You had your friends around.'

'You're one of my friends,' Harriet said. Then her voice trailed away. 'Or...you were...'

This time Jack turned his head. 'I still am, Harry.' But his tone held a note of wariness. 'If you want me to be, that is.'

For a long minute, Harriet stared, unseeing, at the industrial buildings they were passing. She could hear echoes of the laughter of shared jokes and the teasing that Jack had been such a master of. She could feel the warmth of the kindness that was so much a part of him. Like the way he would always make sure that others were being cared for during any breaks on an exhausting disaster response and getting some rest and food and water.

And it hadn't been just his teammates or other people he cared about.

'Do you remember that last callout we were on together?'

'The bush fire?' Jack blew out a breath. 'Sure do. That was a tough one, wasn't it?

A whole town lost. So many people killed or injured.'

'And the animals. You found that dog with burnt paws and you carried him all the way back to base.'

'If I'd known what was going to happen, I would have made you carry him.'

Harriet grinned. 'You mean that photograph of you that went viral?'

Jack shook his head. 'The attention was ridiculous. I started getting emails from all over the country. Girls who'd never met me but wanted to marry me, for God's sake.'

Harriet was still smiling. 'Of course they did. You were a hero. Young, gorgeous and single. And you love dogs. What more could a woman want?'

Jack was concentrating on changing lanes on the motorway that was leading them out of the city. He made a sound that could have been embarrassment at her singing his praises. Or it could have been disagreement.

'You mean you don't like dogs? Or you're not still single?'

'I like dogs,' Jack muttered. 'And, yeah… if you must know, I'm still single.'

Weird, Harriet thought. There must be an unlimited number of gorgeous young women who would love to catch his attention.

Then she sighed into the silence. 'Me, too…'

Jack didn't say anything for quite a while and Harriet could feel a tension that made her wish she'd kept her mouth shut. A lot of it was probably being internally generated, mind you. The rejection of having Pete walk out on their relationship had been soul destroying. She was damaged now. Unattractive. Unlovable, even?

Yeah…she was single and that wasn't about to change. Maybe it never would.

'I heard that Pete transferred to a Melbourne station,' Jack finally said. His tone was laced with disapproval.

Was that what some of the tension was about? Jack had been friends with Pete. Everybody had been.

'Mmm…' Harriet tried to keep her tone

casual. 'I think he wanted a fresh start. With Sharleen.'

Jack shook his head. 'Yeah, I heard about that too. I can't believe he walked out on you. What a moron.'

'It's okay,' Harriet said. Though the aftermath of that breakup had been agonising, she'd refused to let it drag her down further. 'Everything we'd had in common was gone and he just couldn't handle it. And then there was Sharleen. With two good legs. A top surfer. A gym bunny. That was where they met—at the gym.'

Jack took the exit that was signposted for the Kookaburra park and walkway. 'You've still got two legs,' he said, matter-of-factly. 'And, from what I heard, that was a pretty big deal.'

'Yeah…' Suddenly the fierce ache in her leg seemed much more bearable. 'I know. I was lucky.'

'And they must be pretty good legs if you got yourself down that cliff today. I would have thought twice about attempting that.'

'You don't know how dodgy it was. And

I'll probably be reminded of it for a few days now, I expect. I might have to admit defeat and use my brace again at work for a while.'

'You didn't even have a rope.' Jack's glance was one of admiration. 'Weren't you scared?'

'I didn't give myself time to think about it. I just looked one step ahead for a foothold or for the next branch that might give me a safe handhold. And then I was past the halfway point and it would have been just as hard to go back as it was to keep going.'

'But you chose to keep going.'

'I was worried that Eddie might start moving and roll off the ledge.'

'So you gave yourself the biggest physical challenge you've had in a long time and put yourself in danger to save someone else.'

Harriet tried to smile but she could feel her lips wobble. 'It made me feel like… like I was still part of the team.'

Jack was slowing the car now to pull into

the parking area at the park, which was the entry point to the cliffside walkway. He stopped, turned off the engine and then turned to give Harriet a very direct look.

'You *are* still part of the team.'

'Don't be daft.' The fact that his words opened an emotional wound that had barely begun to close up made her tone sharp again. 'That's never going to happen and you know it.'

She could hear the edge of bitterness souring a moment that should have been a reconnection. A step back into a friendship that could be an important bridge between her old life and this new, difficult one.

'Sorry.' The apology came out as a sigh. 'There I go again, being not nice to be around.'

Jack shrugged. 'You're allowed to be angry. I get it.'

'I'm dealing with it. I hope... And I've got my next goals. Two of them, in fact.'

He nodded. 'Like going down the cliff,

huh? Just look as far as the next step or a safe handhold?'

'Something like that.'

'So what are they—these goals of yours?'

'Well, you know that Blake and Sam are getting married, right?'

'Yeah…' Jack grinned. 'So much for Blake's rules about team members not hooking up. He's changed, hasn't he?'

'He's in love. They both are. Sam's my best friend and I'm thrilled for her. I offered to take photos at their wedding but it turns out that I'm going to be her bridesmaid. So that's my first goal. I don't want to be taking any attention away from her by limping down the aisle.'

'The aisle?' Jack's eyes widened. 'They're getting married in a church?' His grin widened. 'I don't believe it. Our maverick ED consultant who wears cowboy boots and a ponytail to work is going to do something as conventional as getting married in a church?'

'They haven't decided where yet. It was

a figure of speech. It might happen on a beach and sand is even harder to walk on.'

'How long have you got to train for it?'

'I don't know that either.' The parking area around them was dark now but Harriet could see some people moving off to one side. 'You'll be coming to the wedding, won't you?'

'If I get an invitation, sure.' Jack had turned to look in the same direction as Harriet. 'So what's your other goal? You said you had two.'

'I want to get back to my old job. In intensive care.'

'Where are you now?'

'Geriatrics.' Harriet screwed up her nose. 'I mean, I love the oldies. I hear the most amazing stories every day but I really miss the ICU.'

'Why can't you work there again now?'

'My leg's not strong enough. Imagine if there was an emergency and I turned to grab a defibrillator or something and I ended up falling over.'

'Hmm…' But Jack seemed distracted. 'There are cops over there. With a dog…'

'Oh…' Harriet wrenched at her door handle. 'It must be Harry the dog. Let's go and check that he's okay.'

The two police officers were about to load Harry the dog into their car but were happy enough to stop and chat when they learned of Jack and Harry's connection to the unusual job they'd been dispatched to.

'You never know what's going to happen on a shift,' the young officer said. 'We get a good hike up a hill in a glorious sunset and we're getting paid for it. How great is that?'

'Was he hard to find?'

'No. He was just lying there, with his nose on his paws, right on the edge of the cliff.'

'Oh…poor Harry.' Harriet crouched down to hug the dog. 'It'll be okay,' she told him. 'Someone's going to look after you.'

'He's going to the pound,' the older offi-cer told them. 'We've tried to find a family member to take him but there doesn't seem to be anybody.'

Harriet felt the nudge of a cold, damp nose against her hand. He was good at communicating, this dog.

'I'll take him,' she heard herself saying. 'I don't want him to go to the pound. How scary would that be? He'd think he was being totally abandoned.'

'If you want to.' The police officers exchanged a glance. 'Can't see a problem with that as long as we get all your details.'

'Are you sure?' Jack sounded concerned. 'He's a big dog. He'll need a lot of exercise.'

Harriet straightened. 'A lot of exercise is exactly what I need, too, if I'm going to get to where I want to be.'

'Are you allowed dogs in your apartment?'

She shrugged. 'Sometimes it's better to apologise later than ask for permission first. I think this is one of those times.'

Jack's gaze was thoughtful. 'I could help, maybe. With the exercising?'

'Sure.' This time, Harriet wasn't going to brush off Jack's offer to help. It was like another peace offering. 'That'd be great.'

A few minutes later, Harry the dog was installed on the back seat of Harriet's car and she was ready to drive home as soon as Jack let go of her door so that she could close it.

'I'll be in touch,' he said. 'We can make up a roster and I can give him a good run on the beach or something.'

'Okay. I'd better get going, though. I need to get to the supermarket and stock up on some dog food and stuff.'

Jack closed her door but he was still standing there so Harriet rolled the window down.

'What?'

He shrugged. 'Nothing. Just that I reckon you could add a third goal to that list.'

'Oh?'

'Yeah...' He threw a smile over his shoulder as he walked away. 'Getting back on the team for real. Reckon you could do it if you really wanted to.'

CHAPTER THREE

'SAM…WHAT ARE you doing here?'

'I had to come and find you. They told me on the ward that you'd brought someone to X-Ray.'

'Yes.' Harriet glanced sideways to where the patient she was accompanying was already snoring gently. 'Poor old May fell out of bed during the night. She's not complaining but it looks like she's fractured her neck of femur. We've got a bit of a wait, though.' She raised her eyebrows at her friend. 'Why did you have to come and find me? Have you set a date for the wedding or something?'

Sam shook her head, flopping into the seat beside Harriet. 'No…it was too late to ring you by the time I got home last night. There was an SDR meeting and I heard all about your cliff rescue. Oh, my God, Harry…what did you think you were *doing*?'

There was only one person who could have been spreading that news but Harriet wasn't entirely sure whether she was disappointed in Jack for talking about her behind her back or quietly pleased that the team now knew all about it.

'Jack said it would have been an astonishing thing for anyone to do but for *you* to do it was just mind-blowing.' Sam was looking down at Harriet's leg. 'Are you okay? You're wearing your brace again.'

'Just a precaution.'

'Maybe you should have an X-ray after May.' Sam glanced at the elderly woman and then caught Harriet's gaze. There was amusement at the snoring but also sympathy. To sit and wait without even conversation was so very different from the challenges of nursing in the intensive care unit.

'I'm fine. Honestly.'

'Better than fine, from what I heard. Jack reckons you should be back on the team.'

Harriet shook her head sharply. 'Not going to happen.'

'Why not?'

'Because I couldn't do it, that's why. You know the kind of things that go with a callout. Tramping miles into the scene of something like a flood or a landslide. And remember the Urban Search and Rescue course that you did? I still have enough trouble walking on a flat surface. I couldn't climb over a pile of rubble after an earthquake if my life depended on it.'

'You just climbed down a cliff and it was only someone else's life that was depending on it.'

'But *I* couldn't be depended on and that's like the number one requirement of an SDR team member.' Harriet wanted to change the subject. 'So, *have* you set a date for the wedding yet?'

Sam groaned. 'We mentioned that we might prefer a beach wedding and now my dad wants to fly everybody off to a tropical island up north. Hamilton or Fraser Island, maybe.'

'Wow… How cool would that be?'

'It would be outrageous.'

'I'll bet Blake hated the idea.'

'My dad's not stupid.' Sam shook her head. 'He offered to donate the same amount of money he would spend on the wedding to *Médecins Sans Frontières* because he knows how passionate Blake is about helping to provide medical care in developing countries. Did I tell you that we're thinking of getting a posting next year? Just for three months or so. Maybe in Africa.'

But Harriet was distracted by the idea of a luxurious island holiday that would be a part of her bridesmaid's duties.

'So it might happen, then? An island wedding?'

'Well, Blake did have a funny look on his face when he said that his mum had never had a tropical island holiday in her life.'

'What's his mum like?'

'Lovely. Tough. She's still struggling to come to terms with her limitations after the stroke.'

'We'd have a lot in common then.'

Sam's face creased into serious lines. 'You're doing amazingly well, Harry. Better than anyone expected. Better than you expected, I would think. Could you have imagined yourself scrambling down a cliff a few months ago?'

'No way…'

'You should have heard Jack singing your praises. He really does think that you could come back on board. If you want to, that is…'

Harriet shrugged, turning to check on her patient. She smoothed white, fluffy hair back from May's face and the old woman stirred and groaned softly.

Being part of the team wasn't an option, she knew that. But, oh…the pull was there, wasn't it? The longing…

'Maybe one day,' she murmured. 'When I'm capable of doing everything that I could do before the accident.'

Which would be never.

'Perfection is overrated,' Sam said. 'We're a team and everyone brings something a bit different to the overall performance. You could still contribute a lot more than you're giving yourself credit for.' She was chewing her lip now. 'And… and you wouldn't have to worry about seeing Pete there any more.'

'I'm not worried. I don't hate him, Sam. I understand that it would never have worked out.' Harriet managed a smile. 'Turns out that broken hearts heal faster than broken legs. Who knew?'

'Mmm… Still, I couldn't believe it when I heard what you'd done. You must be so proud of yourself.'

'You know what? I think I am.' The warmth of the internal glow she was still aware of wasn't just due to hearing that Jack had been singing her praises. Harriet *was* proud of herself. Proud of her leg standing up to the challenge and of overcoming her fears enough to challenge herself that much.

'I just wish someone had got a photo of that.'

Harriet laughed. 'Maybe I should have fished my new camera out and taken a selfie halfway down the cliff.'

'Oh, my God...' Sam's jaw dropped.

'What?'

'I've just had the most brilliant idea.'

'What's that?'

'That could be your contribution to the team—until you're ready for the whole deal. You could be our official photographer.'

'No...' The suggestion made Harriet cringe more than a little. 'That would be like going on a ride-along in an ambulance. Being a thrill seeker who just gets in the way.'

'Didn't sound like you got in the way on that ledge. Jack said you were right back in the swing of things, helping with the gear and the splint and everything.' She was looking thoughtful now. 'Bet he would have loved a photo of winching that guy up to the chopper.'

A distressed sound made Harriet's head turn swiftly. May's pale blue eyes were wide open. And frightened.

'Oh, where am I?' Her words were trembling. 'What's happened?'

'It's okay, May.' Harriet took hold of her hand and stroked it with her thumb. 'We're in X-Ray. You've hurt your leg and we need to find out if something's broken. I'm here with you. You're safe.'

'I hurt my leg? How did that happen?'

Sam was looking at her watch. 'I've got to run. My lunch break's over in two minutes.'

Harriet could see an X-ray technician heading towards them. 'And it looks like it might be our turn. I'll call you later.'

'Yes…do that. I haven't even asked about the dog yet. Is it true that you've sneaked him into your apartment?'

'Shh…it's a secret.'

'Don't think it'll stay that way. Kate already knew.'

'That's because her great-aunt Alice is letting him out for me when I'm at work.

And she and Angus took him out yesterday because they had a day off.'

Sam was on her feet and already heading for the doors of the X-Ray waiting area. 'Just yell if there's anything I can do to help. Like taking him for a run.'

'Thanks, but Jack's coming to give him a good run on the beach tonight. It's all good.'

'We're going to the beach?' May sounded thoroughly confused now. 'I don't mean to be rude, dear, but I don't like sand.'

Harriet smiled, standing on the pedal to release the lock on May's bed. 'Don't worry, May. Not you. It's Harry the dog who's going to the beach.'

She could see that she'd confused her elderly patient even more now but fortunately she didn't have to explain the odd coincidence of having the same name as the dog. The X-ray technician was holding May's hand to check her ID bracelet.

'Just the person we've been waiting for.' His smile was cheeky. 'Are you ready for your photoshoot, Mrs Greene? You look like you're ready to start your modelling career.'

May perked up and seemed to become far more aware of her surroundings. Was she actually batting her eyelashes?

'I like that young man,' she whispered to Harriet as he went ahead to open the doors to the X-ray room.

Harriet grinned. 'I think he's a bit young for you, May.'

May tutted. 'When you're as old as me, dear, you'll realise that it doesn't matter. Age is just a number.'

Harriet was still smiling as she pulled on a lead apron so that she could stay close to May and make sure she didn't move. She might be determined to get back to her more exciting position in the ICU but moments like these—when you got a glimpse of the personalities within these frail old bodies—were a joy.

Harry the dog clearly adored the beach.

As soon as he was let off his leash, he ran straight into the surf, barking in excitement. Jack had a moment of alarm when the black head vanished beneath the foam of a breaking wave but then he reappeared to bound out of the water, pausing only to shake himself vigorously before heading back in.

'I'm tempted to have a swim myself.'

'Go on, then.'

'Will you come in, too?'

'Are you kidding? I'm not in my bathers.'

'You're in shorts, same as me. I reckon they'd be pretty much dry by the time we walk back to your apartment.'

'I only came to watch. And to see how hard it is to walk on the sand. This is the first time I've been on a beach since the accident.'

They'd already come through some soft sand after the grassy area with its picnic tables and barbecue areas that separated this small beach from the road that led back to her apartment block.

'How hard is it?'

Harriet didn't meet his gaze. 'The jury's still out. If you go and have a swim, maybe

I'll take my brace off and see how I go.' She flashed him a wry smile. 'That way, you won't see if I fall flat on my face.'

There was something more than trepidation in that smile. It was more like… embarrassment? About being seen to try something and fail, or was it more than that? Whatever it was, Jack could read the signal.

'You're on.' He kicked off his jandals and stripped off his T-shirt, leaving them beside where Harriet was sitting. Then he strode towards the water, pausing only to pick up a stick of driftwood that looked like something a dog like Harry would love to chase.

He'd been astonished to hear that admission that this was the first time Harriet had been on the beach since her accident. Even during the period that she'd relied on crutches, the distance between here and her apartment would have been manageable.

Everybody knew how much she loved the beach. She hadn't been a competitive surfer, like Pete, but he'd seen the way her face used to light up when she talked about the thrill of riding waves. And she'd been part of the surfing community. Competition days had been exciting events on her social calendar and she'd been very supportive of Pete's ambitions.

Maybe that was it. Maybe she'd been avoiding the beach all this time because it reminded her of the man she'd obviously been head over heels in love with. Why hadn't he thought of that? How insensitive had he been to suggest that she come with him and Harry the dog this evening? Everybody had known how much she'd adored Pete. She'd made light of the breakup of that relationship the other evening but he wasn't convinced that she was over it that well.

How could she be? She'd been living with the guy, for heaven's sake. Committed. He'd been crushed enough when she'd rejected his offer of a date. How much more devastating would it be to have the offer of a lifetime commitment thrown back at you? Did you ever really get over that kind of a blow? Enough to trust anyone with your whole heart again?

Damage like that left scars. And scars could be enough to conceal a very real disability.

The shower of cold water that came as the dog raced to greet him and then shook himself again was enough to break the exercise of berating himself over any insensitivity of suggesting that Harriet come with them to the beach. She had seemed perfectly happy to accept the invitation.

'I'll take some photos,' she'd said. 'That way I can show Eddie how well we're looking after Harry when I go and visit him tomorrow.'

'Great idea,' he'd agreed. 'And I've got a day off tomorrow, too. I'd love to come with you and see how he's doing.'

A glance behind him now showed Harriet with her camera held up to her face and an impressive-looking zoom lens pointing straight towards him. He grinned, holding up the stick of driftwood and pausing for a moment with Harry the dog poised to start chasing it into the surf. That would make a good shot.

There was something a little voyeuristic about staring at people through a camera lens but Harriet didn't feel the least bit guilty.

Jack just happened to be in the same screen as Harry because he was poised to throw a stick for the dog.

But there he was, in nothing but his shorts, with that glorious physique glowing bronze in the low evening sun and the dark swirls of an ethnic tattoo on one shoulder, flowing down to accentuate the muscles of his upper arm.

And that smile! She'd captured that on one shot and knew that it would be an image she'd want to see again. Jack had the kind of smile that could just light up a room. A whole beach, even. It radiated happiness and good humour. Nobody could have a smile like that and not be a really nice person.

She watched them bound into the surf together and then saw the way Harry stayed right beside Jack swimming in water that was way out of his depth. She saw the way Jack kept turning his head to make sure the dog was safe.

He'd be like that when he had kids, one day, she thought. Encouraging them to do things that might be a little dangerous, but he would always be there, right beside them, making sure they were safe. He wouldn't be walking away from his girlfriend or wife if things got a bit tough, either. There was something so solid about Jack Evans and you just knew that your trust wouldn't be misplaced. And friendship *was* something that she could still trust, wasn't it? The real risks only came when you went further than that and she'd never find that kind of trust again. She suspected that it was broken for ever.

Right now, though, that didn't matter. She knew that anything more than friendship wasn't even a blip on any radar that

Jack Evans had regarding her. He was just being the lovely person he was.

He was encouraging her as well. Probably more than he realised. It had actually been a huge thing for her to come to the beach this evening and it felt like she'd crossed a barrier she hadn't even been conscious of erecting. The one that enclosed the old life she had shared with Pete and included the heartbreak of that relationship ending. But here she was and…and it was so nice to be here with the warmth of the sun on her skin and the feeling of sand between her toes and the company of a gorgeous young man who still seemed to want to be her friend even after she'd pretty much dismissed him from her life— as well as a dog who had to be missing his owner terribly but was a shining example of how to live in the moment and make the most of any joy that life had to offer.

So why was she stopping here, just sitting on the sand like a human blob?

Harriet put the cap back on the lens of her camera and slung the strap around her neck. Then she reached down and pulled open the Velcro straps that held her leg brace in place. She pushed herself slowly to her feet and then took a tentative step forward. And then another.

It wasn't easy. But it hadn't been easy getting down that cliff and look how proud she was of that achievement now.

Another step. Harriet knew she was limping badly and could feel a shaft of pain every time she put her weight on her bad leg but she was almost at the water's edge and the temptation to feel the swirl of sea water over her feet was irresistible. Maybe the massaging effect of the dying waves might ease the aches and pains as well.

The first rush of water was cooler than she'd expected and she gasped with the surprise of it. The second wave was bigger and the foam reached her knees and she could feel the sand shifting beneath her feet as the water receded. By the time the third wave had come and gone, it felt like warm silk against her skin and the desire to go further out and swim was as surprising as that first chill of the sea had been.

She wasn't about to go swimming in her clothes, however, and Jack was coming out now, with Harry the dog close on his heels. His face lit up when he saw where Harriet was.

'Feels good, yes?'

Harriet simply nodded but it felt like the smile on her face was wider than it had been for a very long time. She bent to pat Harry.

'It's such fun. I've always envied people who had a dog with them on the beach.'

'You didn't have a dog when you were a kid?'

'No. My parents were older when they adopted me. I think the mess of having a kid around was enough of a shock. I begged for a puppy every birthday but the closest I got was a stuffed toy.' She threw a smile over her shoulder. 'Much cleaner.'

Jack had to slow his pace to let her walk beside him.

'Is the jury back in yet?'

He glanced down at her leg and, for a moment, Harriet had no idea what he was referring to because she suddenly realised just how much he could see.

She'd had jeans on when they'd been on that ledge together. And she'd had the solid brace on for the walk to the beach. This was the first time he was seeing the horrible scarring she'd been left with—not just the angry red marks on her skin but the misshapen muscle from where the initial damage and the complication of infection had destroyed so much of her normal tissue. In fact, it was the first time anyone had seen these scars, other than her doctors and physical therapists. She hadn't even let her best friend see how bad it was.

Her leg was ugly, there were no two ways about that.

She'd looked at it so often herself and cringed at the thought of any man seeing it and still being attracted to her. Not after Pete had almost thrown up when he'd seen it for the first time after the accident. He'd actually dry retched, although he'd tried to cover it up with a cough and he'd avoided ever looking at it directly again. But this was Jack, not someone who could be sizing her up as a potential partner. He was her friend and his query was only concerned with the function of her leg, not its appearance. He was talking about how hard it was to walk on the sand. And, if he could ignore her scarring, then she should at least make a good attempt to follow his example.

'It's definitely harder, but not impossible.'

'That's great.' Jack stooped to pick up the stick that Harry had dropped by his feet. A flick of his arm sent it flying with the dog in hot pursuit. 'We should do it more often, then, and it might get easier.'

'Mmm...' The idea of having company and more visits to the beach was...well, it was really nice. That it had been Jack's suggestion made it even better. He had missed the worst of her struggle to get back on her feet and, after conquering the challenge of that cliff climbing, this felt like a new stage in her recovery. A fresh start.

'The water felt great, too,' she added shyly. 'I might even try a swim next time.'

'Have you been doing any swimming as part of your rehab?'

'No. It took so long for the wounds to heal properly I think it got forgotten. It would have been an infection risk not so long ago.'

'They have those lovely heated pools in the physiotherapy department.'

'I'm an outdoor, cold water sort of person.'

'Yeah... Me, too. But...' A furrow of concern appeared between his eyes.

'But what? You think I couldn't cope in the surf?'

'It's not that. I just think...well, you know what you said about climbing down the cliff? That you just looked ahead one step at a time?'

'What's that got to do with swimming?'

'Before you throw yourself into surf that might be a bit much, why not try one of the salt water pools around here? Some of them have waves that break over the top at high tide.'

Harriet was silent as they arrived back to where Jack's T-shirt and jandals were lying on the sand. He was right. Getting dumped by a big wave could be disastrous and might set back her recovery or even break a bone again. She had to remember her limitations and the possible consequences of pushing too hard but the reminder was less than pleasant.

'I'll come with you, if you like.' Jack's head popped through the neck of his T-shirt as he put it back on and that heart-stopping smile was as bright as ever. 'I love the pools.'

'Harry wouldn't be allowed to swim there.'

'He'll probably be able to go home soon. Let's see how Eddie is tomorrow.'

'Okay.' Harriet shook the sand from her brace and eased her leg into it. It was a relief to hide the scars again but not as much as she might have expected. They'd both ignored it, as if it was no big deal, and maybe next time it *wouldn't* be such a big deal. Jack was just a mate. He wasn't her best friend and he wasn't a boyfriend so it really didn't matter to him what she looked like, did it? He didn't work with her so what she was, or wasn't, capable of doing as well as she once had wasn't important to him, either. He wasn't judging her.

Perhaps that was what was making his company so easy. It seemed perfectly natural to be meeting up to take a dog for a walk like this or to be making arrangements to go somewhere together tomorrow.

No big deal.

Just…nice…

'Oh…that's such a great photo.' Eddie's eyes looked suspiciously bright as he unwrapped the framed image of Harry in the surf, poised to chase the stick that Jack was holding.

'He loves the beach.' Jack's grin was exactly the same as the one Harriet had captured in the photo.

'It's a real treat for him. Hey... I can't thank you guys enough for taking care of him.'

'He's a great dog,' Harriet said. 'I'm loving having the company. I've been living on my own for a while now so it's been a treat for me, too.'

The swift glance from Jack made her realise how easily he picked up on what wasn't being said. That he knew that Pete had moved in with her before the accident and that the toughest part of her recovery had been made that much harder by being left alone to deal with it.

'I always wanted a dog when I was young,' she added hurriedly. 'And everybody else loves him, too. I have a friend, Kate, who's a surgeon at Bondi Bayside, and her great-aunt, Alice, lives on the same floor in my apartment building. She's been taking Harry out during the day when I'm at work.' She eyed the heavy cast on Eddie's leg. 'Will you have someone to help after you get discharged tomorrow? I could keep him a while longer, if it would help.'

'It's all good,' Eddie told her. 'I have a big back yard that's all fenced and I can just leave the doors open all day. It'll only be a few weeks until I can get mobile again. And my neighbours will help. There's a lad down the road who would love to take him for a run.'

'Stay away from the cliffs for a while,' Jack said.

'Oh, I will.' Eddie was still looking at the photograph. 'This is really good,' he said. 'You could be a professional photographer, Harriet.'

'It's become a splinter skill,' she told him. 'And I love action shots.' Her glance slid sideways towards Jack. 'I didn't tell you, but Sam came up with the idea of me going out with the team on the next callout—in the capacity of official photographer.'

'What's the team?' Eddie asked.

'Specialist Disaster Relief,' Jack supplied. 'It's a team of medics from Bondi Bayside plus some extras, like me from the ambulance service and some guys from the fire service. If there's a callout to something big, like a bush fire or a flood or something, we get dispatched as first responders. They fly us in and we've got all the supplies we need to stay for a few days and do whatever we can.'

'Sounds exciting.'

'It is.' But Jack was staring at Harriet with an expression that was almost sombre. 'I think that's a fantastic idea,' he told her quietly. 'Let's make it happen.'

Harriet shrugged, trying to quell the beat of excitement that would make it disappointing if it didn't happen.

'I'll think about it,' she said. 'It'll probably be ages before the team gets deployed again. It's not as if we get disasters every week, thank goodness.'

She hadn't been entirely successful, Harriet realised as they ended their visit to Eddie and drove back to the other side of Sydney.

The excitement was still there.

Growing, even...

CHAPTER FOUR

DESPITE QUITE A few misgivings, this was turning out to be fun.

The SDR team's rare access to the HUET training facility had been the perfect opportunity for Harriet to tag along in the capacity of a photographer. She wasn't taking up extra space in a helicopter or chartered plane and everybody was keen to get a record of one of the more thrilling training sessions that was occasionally available.

HUET stood for Helicopter Underwater Escape Training. After a classroom training session, everybody moved to a deep, purpose-built diving pool dominated by a crane at one side. Attached to the crane was a metal cage designed to replicate the structure and seating of a helicopter. Participants wore float suits that kept them warmer than their normal overalls because they would be submerged more than once. They could take on a vertical escape and one where the 'helicopter' was submerged and then tipped on one side. For the more advanced or bravest amongst the team, they could get tipped completely upside down and even wear blackout goggles.

Harriet was recording everything from the beginning of the session, with people donning life jackets and getting strapped into the harnesses in their seats—even the expressions of trepidation that were obvious despite the dive masks covering half their faces.

She loved the shots she was getting as the cage was swung out and lowered into the pool, with the rush of bubbles exploding around the vanishing figures. She found she was holding her breath as she snapped murky images of the shapes at the bottom of the pool, waiting for people to unclip their harnesses, for someone to open the door and then to see the 'survivors' kick their way to the surface. The grins on faces and thumbs-up signals at that point were a joy to capture.

Harriet hadn't been able to do this training the last time it had been available because she hadn't been able to get time off work but Pete had gone on for weeks about what a thrill it had been and she'd been gutted to have missed out.

She was still missing out, being on the sidelines like this, but it was better than nothing.

Much better.

She could sense the excitement of the others. The fear. The pride in pushing oneself to do something scary and the sheer exhilaration of success. She would have been even more nervous than Kate if she was doing it herself but it certainly wasn't something she could have attempted now. What if she kicked against the metal structure and her leg didn't have the strength to give her the impetus needed to get the door and escape? Someone would have had to help her and that could have put them in danger by making it too long a time to be able to hold their breath.

She snapped a quick series of pictures as Blake climbed out of the pool after the sideways escape and then extended his hand to reach for Sam and help her out. The looks they gave each other were priceless but it might not be one they wanted to share. It was a shared moment of triumph. Total pride in each other and a very deep love.

For a moment Harriet lowered her camera, focusing instead on taking a few deep breaths to counter the sense of loss that swamped her.

Would she and Pete have ever looked at each other like that? It was an irrelevant thought because Pete was long gone but the longing was still very real. Not for Pete but for *someone* who would look at her as if nothing else in the world could ever be that important. That cherished.

And the sense of loss wasn't just due to the empty aftermath of a failed relationship. She shouldn't be standing here, dry and safe, while her teammates were literally immersed in this training session. She still felt like a part of this team and the longing to be properly involved was just as powerful as the need to be loved.

At an even deeper level, it brought back feelings of not being cherished as a child. Not the way that the parents of her friends seemed to love their children. In later years she'd wondered if she'd been added simply to complete a picture of a family. That maybe she'd been a disappointment of some kind. Too messy—the way a dog would have been? Or a sibling?

Maybe being here hadn't been such a great idea after all.

'That was terrifying,' Sam told her, as she came closer.

'You did it, though. Well done. I've got some great photos.'

'Ooh…let me see…'

'Later. I don't want to miss any of the next one. It's the biggie, isn't it? Upside down?'

Sam shuddered. 'Not for me. I've had enough. I'm freezing.'

'Are you heading for the showers?'

Sam shook her head. 'I can't go yet. Not until I know that Blake's out of the pool.'

'He's going to do it?'

'Yeah. And Jack. One of the firies said they wanted to but I think he's changed his mind after the sideways one. I think he swallowed a bit of water.'

Harriet's gaze shifted to where the two men were climbing back into the cage. Lifting her camera was an automatic shield as much as a desire to capture every moment of this experience. It had been Jack, with Sam's backup, who had made this possible and, even if there were painful moments of loss to deal with, Harriet knew she was a whole lot closer to being the person she used to be and that had to be a good thing. Eventually, anyway...

Was Jack nervous? She zoomed in on his face and it felt like he was aware of her watching him because he turned his head, lifted a fist with his thumb up like a flag of confidence and grinned at her.

He had the most amazing smile. Harriet put her camera into video mode. She wanted to give Jack a record of every second of this.

The cage lurched as it was lifted and swung over the water. Harriet's heart lurched right along with it. This was dangerous. No wonder Sam was standing there, hugging herself and looking distinctly pale. Jack was only a mate, not the person she was planning to spend the rest of her life with and she was feeling nervous now herself.

In all honesty, she had been missing Jack's company since Harry the dog had gone home to Eddie. When Jack had called to see if she wanted to come and take photographs today, knowing that he was going to be there had tipped the balance in favour of coming.

The cage swung for a moment and then started to tilt. The two men were lying sideways like the last exercise but then the movement continued until they were both hanging in their harnesses upside down. Harriet knew that her video would capture Sam's distressed sound as their heads touched the top of the pool and then vanished.

She was holding her own breath now as the cage slipped into the effervescence of the escaping air bubbles. Did being upside down make it harder to follow the rules they'd learned in the classroom, to wait until all those bubbles had cleared before they released their harnesses and opened the door?

Surely it was taking too long? Harriet was already starting to fight the urge to suck in some more oxygen but there was no sign of any movement from the bottom of the pool. Sam had her hand pressed against her mouth and the rest of the team looked frozen as they waited. And stared at the surface of the water. Had the men had difficulty with unclipping their harnesses or opening the door? Or had they become disoriented and couldn't kick towards the surface? One of the instructors dropped to a crouch on the edge of the pool. Was he wondering whether he needed to dive in and help?

The tension escalated until Harriet's hands were starting to tremble as they held the camera. Was she about to record a rescue attempt? Or worse…had she snapped the last smile the world would ever see from Jack Evans?

No…suddenly she could see blurry shapes that were moving underwater and almost instantly a head appeared. And then another. It had been a good decision to take a video, after all, because it captured the cheer that came from the whole team and the handshakes and congratulatory hugs that came from every direction as Blake and Jack hauled themselves out of the pool. It was possible it had also recorded the sound she'd made herself. A sigh that expressed the most profound relief that she'd ever felt in her life.

The session broke up a short time later with everyone heading for the showers and changing rooms. Except for Jack, who came over to where Harriet was sitting in the first row of the tiered seats.

'How was that?'

'Awesome. Were you scared, doing that upside down bit?'

'Of course.' But Jack was smiling. He was also dripping wet and had to be cold and exhausted but he sat down on the plastic seat beside Harriet. 'You'd be a bit stupid not to be scared doing that but I figured it was a good thing to try. If it ever happens for real, maybe I'll be a bit less scared and I'll remember what to do.'

'I took a video.'

'Great… I'll look forward to seeing it.' His smile faded. 'How was it, really? Did it make you feel like you were missing out?'

Harriet looked away in case he could see too much in her eyes.

'A bit,' she admitted.

'So how would you feel about giving it a go?'

Her gaze flew back to meet his. *What?*

'I had a chat to our instructor, Chris. He

knows your story. He—and the guy oper-
ating the crane—are both happy to stay a
bit longer. Just for a vertical dip. Just you
and me. Nobody else has to know about it.'

'But...' Harriet was dumbfounded.
'But...*why*?'

'Because this type of training doesn't
come around too often and you might find
yourself back on the team before then and
feel like you missed out on something important.'

Harriet found herself shaking her head
slowly. 'I don't think I could, Jack...'

'Hey...' His tone was firm enough to still
the negative movement she was making.
He leaned closer and held her gaze. 'I believe in you, Harriet Collins. I think it's
time for *you* to start believing in yourself
again.'

He reached out and took hold of her
hand.

'I know how hard it can be to take that
first step,' he said quietly. 'But you're not
alone. I'm here. I can be here for every step
it takes to get you back to where you want

to be. If you want that,' he added, his lips curving into a smile. 'Kind of like a personal trainer.' He gave her hand a quick squeeze and then let it go. 'Or maybe just a good friend.'

The wave of emotion was threatening to drown Harriet. She didn't recognise what it was that was so huge, however. Was this what real friendship had at its core? She could sense that closeness that came with special friends, like Sam, for instance, where you could always count on loyalty and support. But this was different.

Bigger.

Was this what real family was about? The bond of unconditional love that could be there from parents and siblings? From the kind of family she'd never been lucky enough to have herself?

That had to be what was so big it felt it could explode in her chest. What was threatening to bring tears to her eyes. Yes…if she could have had a brother, she would hope he would have been exactly like Jack.

She swallowed hard. 'You really think I should do it?'

'I know you should.' He stood up. 'Come on, let's not keep these guys away from their well-deserved beer for too much longer. There's a float suit waiting for you. You can put it on in the life jacket cupboard and that way nobody else will know what's happening and hang around to watch.'

Had he pushed Harriet too far?

She looked suddenly small, strapped into the seat in the cage beside him. Small and frightened and so, so vulnerable.

This was a much bigger deal for her than for any other members of the team but he'd talked her into giving it a go and here she was.

Trusting him.

As the cage lurched and slipped into the water, he reached out and took hold of her hand.

'Deep breath. Hold it until we're out. Don't worry. I'm not going to let anything happen to you.'

Trust was a precious gift and he wasn't going to let her down.

Good grief…had he really believed that he could keep himself safe from offering anything to Harriet that could put him at risk of being rejected again? He'd done it again, hadn't he, by offering to be a personal trainer and to spend as much time as it took for her to start believing in herself again?

But it still felt like something he was prepared to do. Wanted to do, very much, in fact. He might be shifting the barrier that had been there as far as a real friendship was concerned but he could still protect himself by making sure he didn't let himself hope for anything more than that. Friends were important, too.

Right now, as the cage sank below the surface and kept going down, he wanted nothing more than to protect this woman and the feeling was so strong it felt like it could last a lifetime.

But friendships could last that long, couldn't they? From what he'd seen happening around him, they often lasted far longer than relationships or even marriages. And trust was a two-way street. If she was prepared to trust him *this* much, he had to let himself trust her as well—at least as far as being true friends.

More importantly, Harriet needed to learn to trust herself and not depend on him and he had to trust himself to know where that balance was. She needed a push, as long as she had protection nearby. So he let her hand go when the cage finally stopped its descent. Let her find the buckle on her own harness and release it and then pull herself clear of the cage to kick for the surface.

He couldn't resist touching her again when they reached the edge of the pool, however. Putting his arm around her shoulders and pulling her close for a hug.

'See? Wasn't that bad, was it? Want to try a sideways one?'

Shooting a few hoops on the basketball court was supposed to be a fun way to end an intense workout session at the gym but when you were playing with Blake Cooper, it was an extra workout.

Jack grabbed his towel to mop the sweat from his face and neck and then picked up his water bottle.

'You're killing me, mate…'

Blake grinned. 'Keeping you in shape, more like. You can thank me later.' He took a long pull of his water and then wiped his mouth with the back of his hand. 'While you're in a weakened state, though, I've got something I wanted to ask.'

'Oh?' Jack had something he wanted to ask Blake, too. 'Shoot.'

'We've set a date for the wedding. Two months from today. On Hamilton Island.'

'Wow…' But Jack's jaw dropped. Blake Cooper getting married in an exclusive island playground for the rich and famous? It didn't fit, somehow.

Blake's face acknowledged the reaction. 'Yeah, yeah… I know. But it's for Sam, you know? Or rather her family. She's the only kid they've got left and money's no object.'

Jack put his water bottle down and picked up the ball. 'Guess you'll have to grin and bear it, then. Tough job, but you know…' He bounced the ball and grinned at the SDR teammate and leader who'd become a good friend over the last few years. 'Someone's gotta do it.'

'Glad you understand.' Blake dropped his bottle onto his towel. 'Because I want you to be my best man.'

Jack's hand slipped on the ball and it rolled across the court. *'What?'*

'I need a best man. Harriet's going to be Sam's bridesmaid and…' Blake shrugged. 'I don't have that many good mates. You've got the short straw. D'ya reckon you could put up with a free trip for a weekend? A few hours on a beach, possibly dressed in a penguin suit?'

Someone had caught the escaping ball and sent it rolling back. Jack stopped its track with his foot but didn't stoop to pick it up.

'I'd be honoured, mate. Let me know the details and I'll juggle my shifts if I need to.'

'Hey...' Blake's face was serious as he gave Jack a friendly punch on his arm. 'Appreciate that. Wanna shoot a few more hoops?'

'Sure...' Jack swooped on the ball and bounced it again, this time moving further onto the court. This was the best opportunity he was ever going to get for what he wanted to ask Blake.

'So... Harriet's going to be bridesmaid, huh?' He kept bouncing the ball, ducking away from Blake's attempt to intercept.

'Yep. She's Sam's best mate.'

'She's doing well with her recovery, isn't she?'

'Amazingly well.' Blake grimaced as he missed another attempt.

'She did well at the HUET training last week, too.'

'Sure did. Some of those photos were awesome.'

'No... I meant she did well when she got

in the pool for an escape.' Jack took advantage of Blake's distraction to stop, aim, and send the ball through the hoop after a good smack against the backboard.

'What are you talking about?' This time Blake reached the ball first and was already moving out of Jack's reach.

'After we'd finished, I stayed behind with the crew and we took her through a vertical escape. And then a sideways one.'

'Why?'

'Because she thinks her days of being on the team for real are over.' Jack had his arms up to try and deflect Blake's attempt at a goal. 'It was my idea. Because I don't think they have to be.'

Blake took aim and scored. 'Come on, Jack… You know what it's like out there. There's no way she's going to get up to speed again.'

They both dived for the ball but it was Jack who got there first. He didn't try and run with it, though. He stopped still and tried to catch his breath.

'What would it take?' he asked. 'To prove you wrong?'

Blake shook his head. 'You had enough? Shall we hit the showers?'

Jack wasn't about to let the subject drop. 'How 'bout a five-kilometre hike?' he suggested as they picked up their towels and bottles. 'A hundred-metre sprint or an open-sea swim?' His gaze travelled as they turned towards the exit. 'How 'bout the orange track on the climbing wall?'

Blake was frowning. 'What's this about, Jack? You know as well as I do that she couldn't do any of those things.'

'I reckon she could get there. She's determined enough. Maybe all she needs is the right training programme and a good coach.'

'PTs are expensive. And who knows how long it would take—even if she's actually physically capable of getting there, which I have my doubts about. You saw that injury, man. She's lucky to have kept her leg.'

'As you said yourself, she's doing better

than anyone expected already. And PTs don't have to be pricey. I'd do it for free.'

Blake was about to open his locker. Instead, he turned and stared at Jack.

'You'd do it?'

'Sure.'

'How much spare time have you got, mate? Have you any idea what you'd be taking on?'

'I think so.'

Blake kept staring. 'This is important to you, isn't it?'

Jack turned away from the scrutiny and opened his locker. 'Yep.'

'Why?'

'She's part of the team. We're like family.'

'Haven't you got a real family?'

'Are you kidding?' Jack pulled a clean towel and soap from his locker. 'I've got family coming out of my ears. Aunties and cousins and nieces and nephews. Whole tribe, like any good Island family.'

'But you want to help Harry.'

Jack paused as he was turning away. 'Yeah...'

She hadn't had that kind of family, had she? He hadn't known that she'd been adopted but it had been more shocking to learn that she hadn't been allowed to have a dog. It was heartbreaking to wonder just how lonely she might have been as a child and that only made him more determined to help her now, if she'd let him.

Blake followed him to the showers. 'You've got a big heart, mate. But...'

'But what?'

'Don't go getting her hopes up too much, okay? Keeping her off the team if she's not up to it is for her safety as much as anything else.'

Jack nodded. 'But...you'll keep an open mind? If she *can* prove herself, you'd consider putting her back on the roster?'

Blake shrugged. 'Sure. I'd be stupid not to. She used to be one of our best.'

Jack put his face under the spray of water, letting it sluice the sweat away. He was unaware of the smile on his face.

What he was aware of was confidence that this could happen. With his help, and a hell of a lot of work from Harriet, she could get there.

And, maybe, he wanted that to happen almost as much as she did.

'So…are you up for it?'

Harriet needed to suck in a slow, deep breath. Slow, because it needed to get past a rather large lump in her throat. Deep, because she needed the time to get her head around the enormity of this.

How much time and effort had Jack put into this plan?

He'd set the goals, in order of her own priority. To walk without a limp in time for Blake and Sam's wedding and to be fit enough to go back to her position as an ICU nurse. He'd also added a goal that she'd considered out of reach.

To be an active member of the SDR team again.

He'd also come up with a list of physical achievements that would be enough to convince Blake and the other team committee members that she was capable of meeting any challenges the team was likely to face. Things like long walks, climbing, abseiling and swimming but he'd gone a lot further than that, by making a step-by-step plan of how to achieve an acceptable level of performance without risking injury to her leg.

Spreadsheets. Actual spreadsheets were on the table in front of her in this corner of this trendy beachside wine bar that was close to Bondi Bayside Hospital, and where he'd suggested they meet for a drink after work.

'I can't believe you've done this,' she said, finally. 'It's…mind-blowing…'

'We can get too much downtime when it's a quiet day on the choppers.' Jack reached for his tall glass of lager with a shrug that suggested it wasn't a big deal. 'I'm not studying for anything at the moment so it's been kind of nice to have a project.'

A project? She was a *project*—like a high school assignment?

She could choose to be offended, Harriet realised as her gaze flicked up to catch Jack's.

Or...she could choose to feel...honoured?

There was nothing patronising about the way he was looking at her.

Jack cared. It was as simple as that.

And he *believed* in her.

That statement alone had been enough to get her underwater in that diving pool, strapped into a harness in a metal cage that she knew would soon have several metres of water above it. A place where it was quite possible that her disability could put both her, and Jack, in danger.

But this was bigger than that.

She'd been head over heels in love with her fireman, Pete Thompson, and had been well on the way to happily committing to spending the rest of her life with him until the accident that had marked the beginning of the end of their relationship.

He would never have seen her as any kind of 'project'. In fact, in a blinding moment of clarity, Harriet could see exactly why their relationship had faded into oblivion. Because she had no longer been able to fulfil her role in making his achievements the focus of their life together. She was no longer capable, or even interested, in being his support crew for surfing competitions. Appreciating the dedication he put into keeping his body in perfect shape had gone out the window as well, because it only rubbed salt into the wound of her own imperfections. Without the shared bond of the physical aspects of their relationship, like surfing and sex and the SDR team, there had been nothing left.

That wasn't love, was it?

When you loved someone, it had to go deeper than that. You had to care about someone enough to help them to be the best person they could be, even if it meant sacrificing something yourself.

She would have sacrificed whatever it

took to help Pete if he'd been in her position. But he'd just walked away in the end.

And here was Jack. Just a friend. Not a lover or even someone who'd been an integral part of her life. A friend that she hadn't treated well at all, in fact, but he'd put all this time and effort into a plan to help her regain what she'd lost. To help her become the person she wanted to be again.

Yeah… Harriet caught her bottom lip between her teeth. Blinked a few times to make sure she wasn't going to embarrass herself by shedding tears over the fact that someone cared this much about her.

'Thank you,' she said quietly. 'This is… quite possibly the most amazing thing anyone's ever done for me.'

'So…you're up for it, then?' Jack's smile lit up his face.

'I'll start tomorrow,' she promised. 'With the walking. Increased hill work and then uneven surfaces and soft sand. Ten minutes for the first week and then twenty for the second.' She was tracing the boxes on the spread sheet. 'Good grief…you've even suggested the places to go to for some rocky surfaces or the soft sand.'

'I've used a few of them myself.'

'And I'll re-join the gym.' Harriet nodded. 'And factor in some swimming time.' It wouldn't be hard to find the time. Her life had become rather empty in the hours she wasn't at work.

'I've got my roster here, too.' Jack fished a folded piece of paper from his pocket. 'Let's find at least two or three slots a week that I can work with you.'

Harriet shook her head. 'God, Jack… I wouldn't ask you to do that. You've done enough already. I've got a plan now. My goals are broken down into steps that I can aim for.' She smiled at him. 'I can do this.'

'But I'm your personal trainer, remember?'

'You've got your own life. I wouldn't expect anyone to put that much time into my rehabilitation.' Even if they had chosen to be her life partner. Like Pete. 'Unless I was paying them, of course…'

Jack looked offended. 'I'm not asking to be paid, Harry. I *want* to do this.'

'But…*why*?'

'You're part of my team. Feels like you're part of my family, you know? And we're friends, aren't we? We enjoy each other's company?'

'Yes, of course. But…'

'Stop with the "buts". I like keeping fit myself. We can combine the sessions. Like when you're walking, I can be running. When you're on the sand, I can get a swim in.'

'But what about your social life? I don't want to interfere with that.'

'My social life? You mean my family?' Jack grinned. 'We could make that work, too. Look…' He pointed to a slot on his roster. 'This Saturday here? That's my grandma's birthday and there's a whanau party at a beach that would be perfect for you to swim at because the surf's usually really gentle. We could go early and get a training session in. See?' His grin was triumphant. 'There's always a way to make things work.'

'So I'd be crashing your family party?'

'You haven't met my whanau. Everybody's welcome. Anyway…that's weeks away. We need to get your sand walking skills up to speed before then, what with our weekend away at Hamilton Island on the agenda.'

'*Our* weekend? You've been invited to the wedding?'

'Better than that. Blake asked me to be his best man.'

'Oh…that's brilliant.'

'I know. You and me as the support crew. Team wedding, huh?'

'I've been looking at pictures of the island with Sam to help her choose the wedding venue.'

'There's a choice?'

'Huge choice. There's a yacht club with different decks and a chapel or grassy spots on hilltops. One beach needs a helicopter to get there but I reckon they're going to choose another beach, which looks perfect.

White sand, blue ocean and a backdrop of all the other islands.' Harriet's smile was dreamy. 'It just looks incredible and I can't wait to go.'

'That's that, then.'

'What is?'

'Sand training starts tomorrow. I'll meet you straight after work, okay?'

'You don't have to do this, Jack.'

'I know that. I told you that I want to. Did that rock damage your hearing as well as your leg?'

'Just as long as you know that it's not an obligation. You can stop if it gets to be any kind of a nuisance.'

'Done.' Jack held his drink up in a toast. 'Just as long as you know that the same rules don't apply to you.' He clinked his glass against hers. 'You *don't* get to stop if it's any kind of a nuisance. I may be new at this personal trainer business but I have my standards. If you're in, you're in for the long haul.'

It was that sacrifice thing again. Jack had already done so much by making this detailed plan but here he was offering to give up a significant portion of his free time in the near future to help her try and become the person she used to be—maybe even a better version?

Harriet had to blink again and it was a challenge to find a smile that wasn't stupidly wobbly.

'I'm in.'

CHAPTER FIVE

SHE WAS IN PAIN.

Jack could recognise the signs now, despite how well Harriet managed to conceal it. He could see the crinkles appear at the corners of her eyes or the tiny frown line deepening between her eyebrows. He could hear it by the note of extra cheerfulness that was in her voice.

Most of all, though, he could sense it. As if he was feeling the pain himself and it made it hard to push her that little bit further when what he really wanted to do was…

Was to take her in his arms and hold her for a moment.

To tell her how much he admired her courage. How proud he was of the way she was continuing to face this struggle.

What he *would* do was exactly what he'd been doing for weeks now. He would push her until he knew that she was on the point of admitting defeat and then he would stop the session and let her know that she'd done a great job. Before she uttered anything negative about her current abilities. That point was close now so he was watching her carefully and he saw the briefest hesitation as she gathered her resources to tackle the last, steep part of this hillside track.

He held out his hand.

'Last bit,' he told her. 'We don't want to overdo it.'

Her fingers grasped his and he could feel her letting him take most of her weight as she took the oversized steps these rocks provided.

'We'll stop and rest,' he said. 'And then take the easy route down, nice and slowly.'

Harriet merely nodded, lowering herself carefully to sit on the edge of a boulder.

Jack slipped off his backpack and opened

it to produce two bottles of water and a bag of snacks.

'My sister made this track mix for me,' he said. 'Might have a bit much chocolate in it but there's lots of seeds and nuts and dried fruit as well.'

Harriet picked out a large chunk of chocolate. 'I think I like your sister.' She didn't put it into her mouth straight away. Instead, she closed her eyes and blew out a long breath. 'That was a tough one,' she admitted.

'You couldn't have done it a few weeks ago.'

'I didn't think I was going to be able to do it today.' Her words were slightly muffled by chocolate. 'I almost gave up back there.'

'I know…' Jack caught her gaze as another surge of that pride squeezed his heart. 'But you didn't. Go, you.'

'I would have if I'd been on my own.'

'There you go, then. Having a personal trainer is good for you.'

'Mmm…but is it good for you?' Harriet was reaching for the snack bag.

'Are you kidding? I probably wouldn't have come out at all this morning. It was a bit of a big night last night.'

'Oh?' Harriet grinned at him, another piece of chocolate poised in her fingers. 'Who was she?'

Jack focused on getting a handful of nuts and fruit from the bag. The question was… what…annoying?

'Nothing like that,' he muttered. 'It was a birthday party for one of the firies on the team. Dan?'

'Oh…' Harriet's tone had changed. It sounded almost wistful. 'He was Pete's best mate on the station.'

Was she disappointed that she hadn't been invited?

'It was just a barbecue at the station. Mostly the guys. Too much beer.' Jack's gaze slid sideways but Harriet wasn't looking at him. She was licking some melted chocolate off her fingers.

It was just as well she wasn't looking at

him because he suddenly found he couldn't look away. He hadn't bothered really trying to nail how her question about a female companion had made him feel. He certainly wasn't going to even start analysing what watching her lick her fingers was doing to him.

Man…this woman wasn't just courageous. She was…*hot*…

He needed to shore up that barrier between this friendship and anything else. Anything like the kind of thing he'd once dreamed of. It wasn't going to happen. He wasn't even going to think about the possibility of it happening.

'Did they say anything about Pete?' Harriet asked. 'Has anyone heard from him?'

Okay…this turn in the conversation was disturbing. Was Harriet still in love with the guy?

'Do you really want to know?'

She shrugged, making it no big deal. 'Just curious, I guess.'

'So he hasn't been in touch with you since he left?'

Harriet shook her head.

'Not even to see how you're doing? Or to apologise?' The burn of anger was uncomfortable. Jack got to his feet to shift it. 'And, no, I didn't hear anything about him last night. I don't think anyone thinks much of the way he treated you.'

Harriet didn't say anything and again he wondered how she felt about her ex. The thought of her even talking to Pete again make him feel sick. But it was none of his business, was it? He'd never been in a relationship serious enough to move in with someone so what did he know? Harriet was older and presumably wiser.

She was trusting him with her friendship and he wasn't about to wreck that by telling her what he thought of her ex-boyfriend.

Or, worse, admitting the way he still felt about her sometimes. Like in that moment when he'd watched her licking chocolate off her fingers.

She needed a rock in her life. A good friend. If she knew how often he wanted to take her hand or hold her in his arms to comfort her, she'd think twice about spending time with him at all. If she knew how it made him feel to see her play with her hair when she tied it back in a ponytail or the intense desire provoked by watching her lick her fingers, she'd run a mile and never look back.

It wasn't going to happen.

He stuffed the bag and his bottle into his backpack and then held his hand out for Harriet's bottle. 'You ready to head back?'

She nodded. 'Feels like we've done enough for today, that's for sure.'

'Yeah…' Jack found a smile. 'More than enough. I hope you won't be too sore tomorrow.'

The day room for the geriatric ward at Bondi Bayside was a lovely place for patients to spend time with their visitors with its comfortable chairs and a view of the beach.

'Fancy a cuppa, Nurse?' The woman pushing the tea trolley through the doors of the day room had a badge that advertised her position as a hospital volunteer. 'We've got cheese scones today and, although I don't want to blow my own trumpet, they're pretty darn good.'

'That's very kind of you.' Harriet smiled. 'I'm just coming in to check on one of my patients but I just might sit for a few minutes after that and a cup of tea would be lovely.'

She could use the hot drink to wash down a couple of her anti-inflammatory tablets and maybe they would kick in a bit faster. Her leg was sore today after that hill climb yesterday but she'd been determined not to go back to using her brace at work.

The patient she was going to see was in a wheelchair at the far side of the large room. Poor old May, who'd broken her hip when she'd fallen out of bed, was still an inpatient and it looked as if she was never going to recover enough to be discharged back to her nursing home. Her son, Bruce, a man in his late sixties, had been an increasingly frequent visitor and he'd thought his mum would enjoy a change of scene today. He'd asked Harriet if he could take her outside to smell some sea air but she'd suggested the day room and a view of the sea instead. May had refused to go anywhere with the nasal prongs that were providing some extra oxygen so Harriet needed to check that she was managing without it.

'There's a cup of tea on its way,' she told May. 'And I hear there's some cheese scones as well.'

'Ooh… I do like a good cheese scone.' May reached out to pat her son's arm. 'You do too, don't you, Bruce?'

'Mmm… I'm not very hungry at the moment, though, Mum.' Bruce pulled a large handkerchief from his pocket and mopped his brow. 'It's very hot in here, isn't it?'

Harriet's gaze shifted instantly. 'Are you okay?'

'To be honest, I feel a bit sick.'

He was sweating profusely and his skin was looking grey. Harriet took hold of his wrist to feel for his pulse but she knew he was in trouble before she realised it wasn't palpable. His blood pressure had clearly dropped dramatically.

'Let's lie you down on the floor,' she said calmly. 'I'm going to get one of the doctors to come and see you.'

Bruce nodded. His hand went to the centre of his chest as he started to move and he gave a low moan.

Harriet was holding onto his other arm to help him down so she felt the exact moment that he lost consciousness and crumpled the rest of the way. All she could do was to stop his head hitting the floor too hard.

'Oh, my goodness,' May said. 'Whatever's happened?'

Harriet rolled Bruce onto his back and tilted his head to make sure his airway was open. She tried to find a pulse again, this time in his neck, putting her cheek close to his mouth and her other hand on his abdomen to feel for any signs that he was still breathing.

He wasn't.

Harriet looked up briefly, to catch the horrified gaze of the tea lady. 'Call for help, please,' she told her. 'Tell them we've got a cardiac arrest here. We need the crash trolley.'

Without pausing, Harriet positioned herself on her knees and began chest compressions. She hadn't done CPR for a very long time now but it felt as familiar as if she'd done it only yesterday. Bruce was a big man and it took real effort to make her compressions deep and fast enough to be effective. She only looked up when she heard the rattle of trolley wheels behind her. It was one of the younger nurses on the ward who was pushing it and she looked terrified.

'Is the crash team on its way?'

'Yes. I pushed the cardiac arrest button.'

'Can I do something to help?' The tea lady was wringing her hands.

'Yes,' Harriet said. 'Take May back to the ward. And ask everybody else here to leave.' She still didn't pause her compressions as she looked back at the nurse.

'Open the defibrillator pack and get the patches out. I'll tell you where to stick them. You'll have to work around me.'

One patch went below the collarbone on the right and the other on the left side of the chest. Harriet kept up the compressions, giving directions to her assistant, and she was well out of breath by the time the machine was switched on and she could pause long enough for any heart rhythm to be detected. Not everybody had left the room, she noticed. And there was no sign of the crash team yet.

'Shock advised.' The voice on the defibrillator's automatic program was clear and calm. 'Push "Charge".'

Harriet pushed the button and listened to the whine that changed to an alarm when the charge had been reached.

'Stand clear,' she said, looking up to make sure no one was within touching range of Bruce, including herself. She pushed the shock button and Bruce's arms jerked, then she positioned herself to start chest compressions again.

'Do you know how to use a bag mask?' she asked her junior colleague.

'I think so. I've practised on mannequins.'

Harriet's heart sank but they were still within the window of time when compressions alone were sufficient. If necessary, she could change her position and do CPR from over Bruce's head, which would mean she could ensure that she could deliver respirations as well, but her arms were tiring and, ideally, there should be a change of personnel to deliver the compressions.

Two minutes and then it was time to try and shock Bruce's heart back into action.

'Stand clear...' she called. This time, when she looked up to check safety, she could see the crash team arrive. A bigger trolley, two doctors and another nurse. 'Shocking now.' She pushed the button and closed her eyes for a moment as she let out a relieved breath.

'Well...look at that.' One of the doctors on the crash team was crouching beside her as she opened her eyes again. 'Looks like we've missed all the excitement. Good save, mate.'

And there it was, on the screen. A little erratic but it was close enough to a normal rhythm.

'I've got a pulse.' The other doctor had his hand on Bruce's neck. 'I'll get some oxygen on.'

It wasn't until much later, when Harriet finally went back to the ward, that she noticed her leg was still aching.

She'd never got round to taking those tablets.

And she hadn't given her abilities, or any lack of them, any thought at all during that emergency.

'May?'

'Oh…no…' Pale blue eyes looked more frightened than she had ever seen them look.

'It's okay, May.' Harriet took hold of her hand. 'Bruce is going to be all right. He's having a procedure called an angioplasty now and that's going to fix the artery in his heart that's blocked.'

'His heart?' May's voice trembled. 'He's had a heart attack?'

Harriet nodded. 'It was enough to stop his heart for a little while, and that's why he collapsed. But we got it going again.' She was smiling now. 'He woke up again and he told me to tell you that he's going to be fine. And that he loves you.'

'Oh…' There were tears pouring down May's face. 'You did that? You saved my son?'

'We did. It was a team effort.' Harriet wasn't about to take all the credit, even though the crash team had made sure she knew exactly what a good job she'd done. The conversation she'd had with one of the doctors as they'd got ready to transfer Bruce on a stretcher had made her feel even better.

'You used to work in ICU, didn't you?' he'd said.

'Yes. I got sent here to recover from an injury. It was supposed to be a bit quieter.'

'Well, you look like you could cope with anything again now. Let me know if you need a reference for getting your old job back.'

Harriet sat with May for a while, until her frail patient finally slipped into a peaceful sleep.

And then she sat there for a bit longer because she was actually officially off duty now and she wanted a moment to get her head around what seemed like turning a new corner in her life.

She *had* coped. And coped well. She was ready to ask if she could be considered for her old position again.

She couldn't have done that a couple of months ago and there was someone she needed to thank for her new level of physical ability.

Jack.

The rush of gratitude was a warmth that enveloped Harriet as she sat in this quiet corner of May's room. It held notes of pride and excitement and a hope for the future that was so strong and positive it was the best feeling ever.

And then it seemed to coalesce into something a little bit different.

A feeling that was all about Jack Evans. She couldn't wait to talk to him and tell him about what had happened today. She wanted nothing more than to bask in the gaze she knew she would be under from those warm, brown eyes.

Told you so, that gaze would say. *I've always believed in you…*

They didn't have another session planned until Saturday and that was days away. Harriet found herself actually reaching for her phone. If Jack wasn't working or busy, maybe they could meet up for a drink or something. Her fingers closed around the phone in her pocket but then she froze.

She remembered this feeling of wanting to tell her news to just one person. Of wanting to be with them so much.

The last time she'd felt like this had been…when she'd fallen in love with Pete.

Which was ridiculous.

She wasn't in love with Jack. This was gratitude, that was all.

But a prickle of awareness was trying to contradict that assertion. Flashes of memories that could be interpreted with a very different slant. Like that evening at the beach with Harry the dog, when she'd noticed how gorgeous his skin looked, glowing bronze in the last sun of the day. The way the tattoo highlighted the muscles on his arm. The way his smile made the world a brighter place.

Another flash reminded her of how it had made her feel when he'd told her that he believed in her and how it had persuaded her to do the HUET exercise. That she'd felt like she finally understood what a real family was all about.

And what about yesterday, when he'd taken hold of her hand to help her up those steps when she'd already pushed herself to the limit? She had welcomed the strength in that hand. The touch of his skin against hers…

Oh…*help*…

It was there, wasn't it? If she wasn't already in love with Jack—and she *wasn't*—the possibility that she could be, in the near future, couldn't be denied. She'd believed that that kind of trust was broken for ever for her, but had he somehow slipped behind her defences?

It had to be stopped. Good grief… imagine how Jack would react? Any girl he would choose for a partner would probably be ten years younger than Harriet. He'd probably have a laugh about it with his mates if he knew and they'd make jokes about toy boys or cradle snatching. Call her a cougar, even?

Harriet could feel colour heating up her cheeks. The phone slid from her fingers and she pushed herself up out of the chair.

Not that she believed Jack would be cracking jokes with his mates, he was far too kind to do that. But he would be disturbed, that was for sure. He would find a way to ease off spending time with her and their training sessions would rapidly become just another memory.

She couldn't let that happen. Not when at least one but possibly both of her goals were within touching distance.

Waiting till Saturday to mention today's triumph was no big deal. If she needed to tell somebody else about it before then, she could ring one of her friends. Like Sam. Or Kate. Or even Luc, now living in Namborra with his wife Beth and stepson Toby. Anybody, as long as it wasn't Jack.

'Sleep tight, May,' she murmured aloud. 'See you tomorrow.'

It wasn't the first time that Harriet had used her camera as a buffer between herself and other people but she hadn't needed it this much since her early days of trying to get herself past that dark time when she'd been sure her life would never be the same again.

This was different. It was a buffer between herself and Jack more than anything. A barrier that she had no intention of stepping past.

He looked so happy in the midst of this

family gathering. Right now, he was playing a noisy game of barefoot soccer with participants who ranged in age from his grandfather, who was a goalkeeper, to some small boys who couldn't have been more than about five years old. A couple of dogs were determined to join in the fun and looked like they were presenting quite a hazard but nobody seemed to mind.

There were other men who were in charge of the barbecues, including a spit roast. There were gales of laughter coming from a group of women who were setting out platters of food on one of the big picnic tables and shrieks of glee from toddlers who were being supervised in the shallows by some teenaged girls. A couple of young mothers were breastfeeding their babies under the shade of a tree.

A few members of Jack's extended family had already been here when they'd arrived at the beach.

'This is my friend, Harry,' Jack had introduced her, as they'd gone past. 'We're going for a swim. Look after her bag, will you? It's got her camera in it and she's going to take some photos of the party later.'

And, as easily as that, she had been accepted and welcomed into the rapidly expanding group. They had no idea that this was a big step for Harriet. She'd been doing a lot of swimming in pools recently but this was the first time to tackle real surf since the time before her accident and she was nervous.

She was nervous of being in Jack's company as well. What if he guessed any of the crazy thoughts that had been going through her head since she'd had that disturbing realisation that she had inappropriate feelings for her personal trainer?

At least he seemed blissfully unaware at the moment. He'd stood beside her as ankle-deep water had rushed over her feet and she'd hesitated before walking further into the waves and his smile had offered nothing but empathy and encouragement.

'It's a nice, gentle surf,' he'd said. 'And I'm going to be right beside you. We'll swim out, catch a wave and body surf in, okay?'

Harriet's voice had deserted her. She'd done this a thousand times before and loved the sensation of the water's power rushing her back to shore but she also knew what it was like to get the timing wrong and to be pushed down and held underwater. How much strength you needed in your legs to get you back to safety.

And then Jack had reached out and taken her hand, as if it was the most natural thing in the world.

'You can escape from a helicopter underwater,' he'd called, as he tugged her forward. 'You've got this.'

They'd waded out further, jumping up to avoid being knocked over by waves breaking at chest height. Jack had let go of her hand as they'd had to start swimming, being lifted up and then sliding down the roll of waves that weren't ready to break. Jack had dived through some of them, popping up beside her like a dolphin, his brown skin glistening and a huge grin on his face.

'This one,' he'd shouted, and Harriet had turned her head to see a wall of water coming relentlessly towards them.

There had been no time to panic. She'd needed to turn and point her body towards the shore. To kick her feet to keep at the front of the wave and then hold her breath as it began to break and cover her in foam as she'd shot forward. Within seconds, she'd been in water that was shallow enough to stand up, salt water streaming down her body.

Jack hadn't paused for any longer than it took to give her a thumbs-up before he'd turned back.

'Good, huh?' he'd called. 'Let's do it again.'

They'd stayed in the water for nearly an hour, catching wave after wave, and it had been the most exhilarating therapy Harriet had experienced since her accident. It was not only good for her body...it was doing something wonderful for her soul. She loved the sea and being in the surf.

And…there was no avoiding the truth now, she loved Jack as well.

So, here she was, hiding behind her camera as she stayed to share in the family celebration of Jack's grandmother's birthday. Having dried herself off after the swim, she was also hiding in her favourite maxi dress with its strappy top and swirly skirt that had a ragged hemline reaching her ankles. Her hair had gone super curly after being soaked in salt water, she had no make-up on and bare feet but it didn't matter. Harriet hadn't felt this happy in a very, very long time.

She was tired and her leg was aching but it was actually a joy to be wandering around capturing candid shots of this huge, loving family. She caught an auntie stooping to kiss and comfort a toddler who'd fallen over. A father laughing up at the baby he was holding above his head. The grandmother who was sitting regally on a beach chair that had been draped with flowers and, of course, the action shots of the fierce but friendly soccer game.

She'd never known what it was like to have a close family and this was completely at the other end of the spectrum. They would just absorb whoever Jack chose as his partner in life, wouldn't they? The wedding would be a huge celebration and someone would always be there to help if they needed a babysitter or something. Their children would have an endless supply of cousins to play with.

A stab of envy dimmed the happy shine of the afternoon for Harriet.

She wanted to be that girl.

And she knew she never could be.

A little later, she had to abandon her camera to sit on the grass with a plate of delicious food. She was amongst a laughing group that included Jack, two of his sisters and several of their children. A sea breeze had picked up but, focused on eating, Harriet didn't notice that she'd lost the safety barrier of more than her role of photographer.

'What's wrong with your leg?' a small boy asked.

'Um…' A glance down showed that her skirt had folded back and her bad leg was completely exposed in all its misshapen glory. Hurriedly, she tugged the fabric free and covered her scars.

'I…um…'

'Harry had an accident.' Jack spoke up from the other side of the group. 'She had climbed down a mountain and then a big rock came down and landed on her leg.'

'Wow…' The boy's eyes grew as round as saucers. 'You can climb mountains? That's *cool*…' And then he turned to his mother. 'Can I have some ice cream now?'

'Go on, then…' His mother ruffled his curls. 'Bring some back for your sister, too.' She smiled at Harriet. 'That must have hurt so much,' she said. 'But it looks like you're recovering well.'

'That's because she's got the best personal trainer around these parts,' Jack put in.

'Says you.' His sister grinned. 'Hope

you're not paying him too much, Harry. I think he just wants an excuse to keep fit and have someone to play with.'

Harriet just smiled. They thought she was paying Jack? That she didn't qualify as being a real friend? Any fragments of longing to be part of a family like this evaporated. She really didn't belong here...

Her appetite had vanished. The conversation moved on swiftly but Harriet wasn't contributing. The return of the little boy, holding two enormous ice-cream cones, gave her the excuse she needed. She scrambled to her feet, ignoring the shaft of pain that trying to look normal doing so provoked.

'That looks really good,' she murmured. 'I might go and find one, too.'

Not that she wanted an ice cream. What Harriet wanted right now was to escape. She had come with Jack, though, so she'd have to wait until he was ready to leave. The best she could do for the moment was to find a rubbish bin for her picnic plate and then wander off down the beach to find a quiet spot to sit for a while.

Minutes ticked past as she watched the waves gather momentum and then break up to roll onto the sand. She heard the sound of many voices singing 'Happy Birthday' and then bursts of clapping as speeches were probably being made. She needed to go back but if she waited a bit longer, maybe the cleaning-up process would be underway and Jack would be ready to drive her back into the city. Had he noticed her absence? Would he be angry at how rude she'd been?

'Hey...' The smile on Jack's face as he walked towards her didn't suggest anything like anger. 'My tribe got a bit much for you?' He flopped down onto the sand beside her. 'Sorry about that.'

'Don't apologise. Your family is lovely. I just...'

'Needed some space. I get it.'

The breeze was tugging at the hemline of her dress again so Harriet held it down.

She caught her breath in a gasp as Jack put his hand over hers and pulled it away.

'You don't need to do that,' he said quietly. 'Don't let your scars embarrass you.'

'They're ugly,' Harriet muttered. 'I hate them.'

For a moment they sat there in silence that was broken only by the soothing sound of the waves. Harriet closed her eyes. She didn't want to see that empathy in Jack's face. But she didn't try and hide her leg again either. He'd seen it before.

The touch of his fingers on her leg was so shocking that Harriet froze. She couldn't even open her eyes.

'I don't think they're ugly,' he said softly. 'I think they add to your beauty.'

Now it was even hard to breathe. Nobody had touched her leg when it wasn't medically required for the longest time. Nobody had touched any part of her body like this for even longer.

As if it was…something special. Something to be honoured.

'It's evidence of the kind of strength you

have, Harry,' Jack continued. 'You should be proud of what you've achieved. *I'm* proud of you...'

It was embarrassing to feel so close to tears. It was worse to open her eyes, see the way Jack was looking at her, and have to fight the urge to lean in and...*kiss* him?

But, dear Lord, he looked as if he was thinking the same thing. As if the only thing he wanted was to kiss *her*.

She couldn't let it happen. No matter how much she longed to be touched the way he had touched her leg, she couldn't do that to Jack. She would be taking advantage of their friendship. Risking losing it even. She was misinterpreting that look, that was all. Making it something she *wanted* to see? He was proud of her and he was invested in her success because he'd put so much time into it himself.

Such a short time ago, she'd thought about the girl who might be lucky enough to become part of his family. Someone a lot younger than herself. Someone who would be introduced as more than simply a 'friend'. Someone who might be used to being part of a real family and wouldn't feel awkward or like they didn't really belong. Whatever the reason, she'd known that it wouldn't be her.

Harriet pushed back at that desire so hard it was enough to get her to her feet.

'Thanks,' she said lightly, pasting a smile onto her face. 'It's just as well your family doesn't know how bad your rate of pay as a personal trainer is.'

She knew Jack was following her. She could also sense that he had been bewildered by her comment and didn't know what to say in response. The silence felt awkward, even when he broke it.

'Do you know, you're walking on sand almost without a limp?'

'Just as well, with the wedding coming up in a couple of weeks.' This was better. A line of conversation that would take them well away from anything too personal and cover up that weird moment when a kiss had hung in the air between them, just waiting for one of them to make the first move. 'Have you been measured up for your suit yet?'

'Not yet. I think that's happening this week.'

'It's going to get busy.' Harriet nodded. 'My bridesmaid duties are hotting up.' They were nearly back to where the party was finally winding down. 'I don't think I'm going to get much time for any training before then.'

She couldn't miss the flare of surprise in Jack's eyes. Or the tiny frown that followed, as if he was drawing a more significant meaning from her words. Then he nodded and turned away.

'No problem. You ready to head back yet?'

'Sure. Let me just go and find my bag.'

They walked in opposite directions. Harriet to gather her things and Jack to say his farewells to his grandmother and other family members.

Harriet could feel the distance between them growing more than physically.

It felt as if they'd been at some sort of

crossroads back there. As if there'd been an offer of something hanging in the air but it hadn't formed enough to be accepted. Or, more likely, rejected. She had chosen to walk away and Jack was respecting that.

It had been the right thing to do.

So why did it feel so very wrong?

CHAPTER SIX

'YOU LOOK *PERFECT.*'

'You think?' Sam glanced over her shoulder at the full-length mirror and just the movement of her head gave the impression that the shimmering fall of her dress was floating in a sea breeze.

Harriet did a quick twirl to make her own skirt float a little, too. 'I would never have thought to wear something yellow but I really love it.'

'It's my frangipani theme.' Sam touched one of the tiny white and gold flowers dotted amongst the soft braids that was an elegant style, just messy enough to be perfect for a beach wedding. 'We chose the fabric of your dress to match the centre of the flowers.'

Harriet dipped her head to sniff the bouquet she was holding. 'They're gorgeous. And so tropical. Perfect choice.'

'I was going to go for gardenias because they smell so wonderful and they look all white and bridal but then I got into re-searching the meanings of the flowers and...' A poignant smile touched Sam's lips. 'I couldn't go past frangipanis.'

'Oh?' Harriet moved towards the silver tray with the flutes of champagne they hadn't touched yet. 'What do they mean?'

'They symbolise intense love and a lasting bond between two people and the strength to withstand tough challenges. The boys have got them in a buttonhole, too. With a little spray of ferns behind them.'

'Nice. I love that.'

Harriet handed Sam a glass of cham-pagne, noting the immaculate French pol-ish they both had, on their toenails as well as their fingernails. They had pretty san-dals to wear so she had submitted to the pedicure in the salon this morning and tried to ignore that her scarred leg was on display. Now she was pleased that she had. Not just because her hands and feet looked so good but because it had been a lovely time, with both Sam and Blake's mothers sharing the pampering. It had felt like family. Not like the exuberant and welcoming gathering of Jack's family on the beach the other week but still close and warm and special.

'Oh… I've got something for you.' Sam pulled a tiny package from her bag. 'It's just tiny but I wanted you to have something to remember today by. I got one for both of us.'

'I'm not likely to forget it. I can't believe I'm even here. Hamilton Island is stunning.'

The gift was a pretty ankle bracelet, a silver chain with tiny ceramic flowers. Frangipanis.

'It's gorgeous. Does it matter which ankle you put it on? Am I going to be advertising my single status or anything?'

Sam laughed. 'I'm sorry it's not a huge

wedding with some surprise guest who's going to sweep you off your feet.'

Harriet was looking down at her ankles. In this long dress, it looked like both her legs were perfectly normal so it didn't matter which one she chose.

What did matter was that she couldn't even think about her ankles or legs without her brain taking her instantly back to that moment when Jack had touched her scars so gently.

When he had pretty much told her that he thought she was beautiful.

When that kiss that hadn't happened had seared itself into her brain. And her heart…

She put the bracelet onto her scarred side. Because she liked the symbolism of withstanding tough challenges.

And the lasting bond between two people. A sharp pang of loss made her catch her breath. She hadn't had either of those things with the man she'd thought she'd been going to marry. But she was over Pete now, she reminded herself firmly. Completely over him. And, in a different way, she had both of those attributes with Jack. A tough challenge that he'd been with her on, every step of the way. And friendship was a loving bond, wasn't it?

If she still had that with him?

She took a long sip of her champagne, unable to answer that question. She hadn't seen him in the last couple of weeks. Ever since that family party at the beach. He'd told her to text him if she found she had any free time and wanted a training session.

She hadn't made any contact at all. They hadn't been on the same flight to Hamilton Island from Sydney and the wedding preparations had meant, of course, that she and Sam were separated from the groom and his best man. She wouldn't see him until she accompanied Sam down the strip of white carpet on the beach to the spot between the palm trees where Blake would be waiting for her, Jack by his side.

Would she even be able to make eye contact with Jack, given the kinds of things she'd been thinking in the lonely hours of the nights since that almost kiss?

A knock at the door interrupted her anxiety. It was Sam's mother.

'I have to go and find my seat in a minute but the photographer wants a few more of the "getting ready" shots. Can he come in again?'

'Sure.' Sam smiled at Harriet. 'Let's get one of our matching ankles.'

'Hey… I'm the one who's supposed to be nervous, not you.'

Jack's smile was wry. 'Guess I'm not used to being in the spotlight. Or in a suit, for that matter.'

'You and me both, mate. But today's for Sam and I wanted it to be perfect for her. I did draw the line at a tie, though.'

'Good thing, too, in this heat.' The open-necked white shirt beneath the cream linen suit was ideal for a beach wedding and Jack felt right at home with sand between his toes and the mottled shade of palm trees overhead. If he ever got married, he'd want a setting like this. His family would all be keen for a trip home to Samoa, wouldn't they? And island parties were the best...

It was unfortunate that any thought of having a wedding of his own or finding a bride inevitably took his thoughts straight to Harriet Collins because that made him fidget again.

He *was* nervous but it had nothing to do with the small crowd of people now settled into the rows of white chairs on the beach. Or that he still had best man duties to perform, like making a speech later.

It had everything to do with the fact that he was going to see Harriet very soon and he hadn't seen or heard from her since that moment on the beach when he'd stupidly given in to the urge to touch her skin in a way that no personal trainer ever should. When he'd had to fight an even more overwhelming urge to kiss her because, for a crazy blip of time, he'd thought she wanted him to.

And now she'd run away. As he'd known she would if he ever took that step closer.

Sure, she'd been busy helping Sam. There must have been all sorts of last-minute details that had to be organised and women had a lot more to do in the run-up to a wedding than the men did. When one of his sisters had got married a while back, there'd been endless discussions about hairstyles and manicures and goodness knew what else.

But how long did it take to send a text message, even if it was just to say that she didn't have time for a training session? He'd deleted more than one message on his own phone before hitting 'send' because instinct told him that if she was avoiding him or running away, chasing her would only make it worse.

'You've lost the rings, haven't you?' Blake had noticed his restless movement again.

'No way. Toby's got them, remember?' He turned his head to smile at the small boy wearing a miniature version of their suits. He was sitting on his mum's lap in the front row on the groom's side of the gathering. His new stepdad gave Jack a thumbs-up signal and grinned.

'I miss having Luc in the team,' he murmured. 'We were a bit remiss in not giving you a stag night, too.'

'Not into that kind of thing,' Blake said.

'No kidding…' Jack's smile was more relaxed now. Blake's hair might be tied back the way he kept it at work in the emergency department but he'd already pushed up the sleeves of his jacket enough to make a personal, casual style statement. It was just as well that casual beach shoes had been deemed appropriate or the groom would probably be wearing his beloved cowboy boots as well.

'And Luc's a family man now,' Blake added. 'Namborra's a bit far to have come to Sydney for a night out. We'll make up for it later. Oh…' His voice cracked as soft music began and every head turned. *'Wow…'*

Jack caught his breath at the first sight of Sam, looking so radiant and beautiful, but it felt like his heart had stopped in sympathy the moment he saw Harriet. She looked like a ray of sunshine in that pale yellow dress and he'd never seen her hair lifted up from her neck like that. With the tiny flowers amongst her curls, she looked almost like a bride herself. He knew that Sam was the star of this show but, for him, Harriet Collins was outshining the bride. Without the slightest doubt, she was the most beautiful woman he'd ever seen in his life.

And…and she wasn't limping. Not even a little bit…

He felt incredibly proud of her at that moment. So proud he had to blink hard to get rid of the extra moisture in his eyes.

Maybe it was just as well she wasn't looking at him. Even when they'd stepped aside so that only the celebrant was framed between the palm trees in front of Sam and Blake, Harriet kept her gaze firmly on what they were here for—the exchange of vows between two people who were making a public declaration of a love they both believed would last for the rest of their lives.

Jack tried to keep his own gaze focussed on Sam and Blake as well and it wasn't hard. The vows they had written were personal and beautiful and little Toby was very cute as he played his part in delivering the rings. But then it came, finally. That moment when they had their first kiss as a married couple and there was nothing Jack could do to stop his gaze sliding towards Harriet.

Had she already been looking at him or had she just felt the same pull at exactly the same moment?

It didn't matter.

The kiss between Blake and Sam had made her remember and, in that long moment of connection when neither of them could look away, Jack knew he hadn't been wrong.

Harriet *had* wanted that kiss on the beach that day.

As much as he had.

They both broke eye contact as the applause from the guests began. They had duties to perform now, like the signing of the register and then the official photo session. He still had his speech to make later, too, but Jack wasn't feeling remotely nervous any more.

He wasn't quite sure what this enormous sensation in his chest was. Relief? Excitement? Pure joy?

Whatever it was, this wasn't the time to think about it. Or to try and talk to Harriet about it.

It was enough that it was there.

And, suddenly, Jack thought he recognised what this huge feeling was.

Hope…

Oh, man…

The way Jack had been looking at her.

Maybe it was a result of the most romantic setting ever, on this gorgeous beach with the background of a turquoise sea interrupted only by the lush green shapes of outer islands and the blue of the sky by some harmless, cotton-wool puffs of cloud.

Or maybe it was a reflection of the palpable love between the two people who had just joined their lives together in the most beautiful exchange of vows Harriet had ever heard.

Weddings were notorious for sparking romance amongst the witnesses and guests, weren't they?

Except that she'd seen a paler version of that look in Jack's eyes before. When he'd touched her leg, as if her scars were a part of her that was as acceptable and important as any other part of her body. She could have drowned in that gaze and it had been a shock when the guests had begun clapping because, for a heartbeat, she'd totally forgotten that anyone else was here. Even Blake and Sam.

She didn't dare catch his gaze again. She busied herself, making sure that Sam's dress was in perfect folds and that the breeze hadn't messed up her hair for the photos as they signed the register and then moved to a more formal photo shoot further down the beach. It was easy to smile at the camera as group shots were taken but it became harder as the photographer suggested some more casual ideas.

Towards the end, both Blake and Jack had discarded their jackets and shoes and rolled up the legs of their trousers so they could stand in the gentle wash of waves.

'Grab your girls.' He grinned, then. 'Hold them up high enough so their dresses won't get wet.'

Blake had no hesitation in scooping Sam into his arms and walking back into the water. She had her arms around his neck and was laughing up at him and then he dipped his head to kiss his bride and Harriet knew it would be the best photo. She was so caught up, watching them, she barely noticed that Jack was right beside her.

'Yes,' the photographer called. 'Awesome. Now we need the whole bridal party in the sea.'

Harriet caught her bottom lip between her teeth. She had to look up at Jack now, to see whether he was feeling anything like she was—as if she was about to take a flying leap off a cliff.

But he was smiling, his eyebrows raised in a query. He liked this idea.

With a tiny sigh, Harriet gave in to the moment, reaching up to put her arms around his neck. She felt strong arms take hold of her and then lift her as he turned and walked into the water.

She hadn't been in a man's arms like this for longer than she could remember. Once, Pete had picked her up on the beach and run into the surf, but only to dump her in deeper water. It had been a game. Fun.

Nothing like how this felt.

Jack wasn't about to drop her and it wasn't just because it would ruin her dress. The feeling of having his arms around her like this suggested a safety that went far beyond any clothing.

She trusted this man. And he was the sweetest, most generous person that she knew. She couldn't do anything that would cause him harm—physical or emotional. He might think he wanted to be with her as more than a friend but she couldn't allow that to happen if it had the potential to hurt him. She might think she was capable of trusting someone again but what if she was wrong? Was she really ready to risk having her heart broken again?

It was a huge thing to contemplate. Terrifying, even.

Not that she could give that fear any headspace right now and spoil this fun. They were all laughing, even when Blake's trouser leg unrolled and got soaked. Their feet were caked with sand as they made their way back to the reception in the yacht club and neither of the men put their jackets back on but nobody seemed to mind. The venue was gorgeous, on an open deck with the fabulous views that were getting more and more stunning as the sun sank. Tables were sheltered by umbrellas that had hanging lanterns that would look like small moons as it got darker. The food was amazing, the speeches all went well and the dance floor was ready for them to party on into the night.

Harriet knew that she would have to dance with Jack, at least once, as they joined the bridal couple after their first dance. She wanted to dance with him so much that it was ringing alarm bells. If he looked at her the way he had during Blake and Sam's kiss, while he was holding her in his arms and moving to soft, romantic music, she would be totally lost. It might be impossible to even remember the reasons why anything more than friendship with Jack wasn't a good idea. That one— or both—of them would only end up getting badly hurt.

That was why she took a moment to have a private word with Sam. To whisper that her leg had reached its limits for the day and that she was scared she might fall on her face if she tried dancing. She saw Sam whispering to Blake a short time later and then Blake got up, resting a hand on Jack's shoulder as he bent to say something to his best man before taking his bride's hand and leading her to the dance floor.

A part of her heart was breaking at

the smile that Jack gave her as he leaned closer.

'No worries,' he murmured. 'You've done so well today, Harry. Not even a limp. We won't push it.'

'Thanks.' She couldn't quite meet his gaze. 'I did it, didn't I? Met my first goal of being the bridesmaid that didn't limp. Thanks to you.'

'I reckon you would have got there without any help from me. I'm just glad I got to go along on the ride.' Jack cleared his throat, reaching for his glass of water. 'How 'bout that other goal, of getting your old job back?'

'I'm getting a trial next week, thanks to that cardiac arrest I told you about. I know I can do it.' But the shine of this new step forward in her life had dimmed. Jack sounded as if their training sessions together were a thing of the past. A 'ride' that was now over. It would make things easier not to spend so much time together but there was a hollow feeling in her stomach that felt a lot like loss.

'I know you can, too.' Jack was smiling again. 'Reckon it's time to talk to Blake about getting back on the team.'

They both turned to watch Blake and Sam as they were dancing. It was clearly something they both loved to do and their dancing was a pleasure to watch. The joy that emanated from the couple made Harriet catch her breath.

'One step at a time,' she said. 'I doubt very much that Blake wants to think about the team while he's on his honeymoon.'

If she joined the team again, it would mean regular team meetings and training sessions on top of any actual callouts. More time in Jack's company, even if the personal training was done. She needed to get her head around that and make sure she could handle it and stay strong. For Jack's sake as much as her own.

The silence felt a little awkward until Jack broke it. 'They're staying on here, aren't they?'

'Yes, for a week. They've got a private bungalow on one of the smaller islands and a line-up of amazing things to do like snorkelling and swimming with turtles. I'll have to come back here one day myself, I think.'

The first dance was ending and Sam and Blake went in opposite directions to find new partners to bring to the floor. Sam came towards the bridal party's table.

'Jack… Blake says I have to dance with our best man.' But her smile faded a little as she looked at Harriet. 'You don't mind, do you, Harry?'

'Go for it,' she said. 'Blake's got your mum up on the floor and look…your dad is asking Blake's mum.'

'He knows about her disability. He'll be gentle.'

They all knew that Blake's mother was limited in her physical abilities after her stroke but here she was on the dance floor, in the arms of a man who would be taking care of her. Beth was there as well and she had problems with her vision but Luc was there to protect her and they had little Toby holding each of their hands and bouncing enthusiastically to the music.

Harriet could feel Jack's gaze on her. Telling her that he would have been gentle as well. That he could protect her. That she could cope if she wanted to.

It was just as well that Sam was dragging him away to join the increasing number of people who were getting up and into the fun. Harriet was left alone at the table. She watched for a few minutes but then stood up and walked towards the end of the deck. Nobody was going to miss her if she took a few minutes to herself and went out to enjoy the shine of the moon on the sea.

'Where's Harry?'

'I have no idea.' Jack had noticed the empty space at the table a while ago but he'd assumed that Harriet was mingling to talk to other guests.

'I thought she'd gone to the loo but I've just been and she's not there.' Sam was looking worried. 'Do you think she's okay?'

'She seemed fine. Apart from not wanting to dance.'

'Maybe her leg's worse than she was letting on.' Blake appeared beside Sam and slid his arm around his new wife. 'Could you go and look for her, Jack?'

'Sure.' Except that he might not be welcome if he found her. This would be chasing her in a far less subtle manner than sending a text message or something. But now he was worried, too.

'Tell her it's no problem if she's tired and needs to go back to her bungalow. We'll see her at the breakfast tomorrow.'

'Will do.'

'And thanks, Jack. For everything. It's been the best day.' Sam stood on tiptoe to plant a kiss on his cheek. 'And now I need to go and dance with my husband again.'

'Call us if there's a problem,' Blake added, but he was smiling down at Sam. 'Husband, huh? How soon can we slip away, do you think?'

Jack paused at the bar at the end of the

deck. 'Have you seen a gorgeous redhead in a yellow dress recently?'

'Couldn't miss her,' the barman said with a wink. 'Looked like she was heading to the beach for a bit of fresh air.'

The sand still felt warm beneath his feet as Jack walked along the beach. The sounds of the party faded behind him until all he could hear was the soft wash of tiny waves. The beach looked completely deserted and he was walking away from the main part of the resort where he could have made enquiries about which bungalow she was in for the night.

Instinct told him that there was a problem. Not with her leg necessarily but… with *him*.

That same instinct told him that Harriet wouldn't have shut herself away in a room. That she probably wasn't far away and that she was finding peace in this soft symphony of sea music and moonlight.

And…there she was, her skirt bunched up in one hand, her sandals dangling from the other, walking close enough to the sea to have her feet covered by foam at the end of every wave.

'Harry?'

She turned. And stopped.

'Sam was worried about you. She sent me to see if you're okay.'

'I'm fine.' Harriet bit her lip. 'I just came out for a minute but…it's so beautiful I guess I lost track of time.' She came away from the water and let the skirts of her dress fall. 'I'd better go back, hadn't I?'

'There's no rush.' Without thinking, Jack put out his hands to touch Harriet's shoulders and stop her moving forward. 'I… I think we need to talk…'

He could feel the softness and warmth of her skin beneath his hands. Her eyes looked huge in this soft light and her gaze was holding his as if she couldn't look away. As if she didn't want to…

A puff of breeze caught a curl of her hair that dangled in front of her eyes. Jack moved his hand to brush it back and then his fingers cupped the back of her head. He could feel the way her head tilted into his hand and his gaze dropped to where her lips had parted. There was no way on earth he could have resisted the force of what felt like a reflection of his own longing. He bent his head and touched her lips with his own.

This was every bit as astonishing as any fantasy kiss that had haunted her nights recently.

Only so much better, because it was real.

That first touch of Jack's lips had been so gentle. So slow and thoughtful, as if he was soaking up something way more than physical contact. Building into an inevitable rush of sensation that she knew had taken them both by surprise because of that brief moment in time where they both froze. A tiny part of her brain registered her sandals falling from her hand before she reached up to put her arms around Jack's neck. And then it was an avalanche of a kiss on a very different level that was sweeping her into a place that felt totally new.

Huge.

Scary, definitely... But it didn't feel wrong. Quite the opposite, in fact.

It was hard to catch her breath when they finally broke apart.

For a long, long moment, Jack held her gaze. And then one corner of his mouth lifted.

'Sorry.'

Her eyes widened. How could anyone be sorry about a kiss like that?

'I didn't ask for permission, did I?'

And then she remembered what she'd said when Jack had asked whether she was allowed to keep Harry the dog in her apartment. That sometimes it was better to apologise later than ask for permission first.

She felt her own lips curve into a smile that just kept growing and any awkwardness between them seemed to vanish. Their friendship was still intact, and it had just stepped onto a completely new level.

A miraculous, totally unexpected level.

'I'm not wrong, am I?' Jack asked softly. 'You're feeling this, too?'

'You're not wrong.' The words were a whisper. Harriet had to close her eyes for a heartbeat. Feeling it didn't quite cover this overwhelming surge of emotion. Amazement and joy. A warmth that only came from love and an excitement that was pure sexual desire. But there was also trepidation mixed in there. Guilt even...

She opened her eyes to find Jack's steady gaze locked onto hers.

'But...?'

'But...it couldn't work, could it?'

'Why not?'

'I'm older than you, Jack. Maybe enough that your mates would laugh at you. People would look at me like I'm a cradle snatcher or something.'

Jack's breath came out in a huff of laughter. 'You're kidding, right? You know how hard it is to find somebody that you feel like this about? What the hell do a few years' difference in age make? Age is just a number. And who cares what anybody else thinks, anyway?'

Harriet couldn't look away from those

dark eyes. He really believed this. Other people probably did, too. She could almost hear the echo of May's voice at the back of her head saying exactly what Jack had just said. That age was just a number…

'Hey…when you're eighty-something and I'm only seventy-five, do you really think it's going to matter a damn?'

Now she couldn't breathe again. This was more than just sexual attraction Jack was talking about, wasn't it? Could he see them still being together when they were that old? Did he really see this as the start of…*for ever*?

Oh…*wow*… Yep. This was terrifying. But irresistible…

'But…but what about your family?'

'What about my family?' A frown creased Jack's brow. 'You didn't like them?'

'I loved them. They're the kind of family I would have dreamed of having as a kid. But…you introduced me as just a friend. They thought I was paying you for being my personal trainer.'

Jack laughed. 'If I'd introduced you in

any way that made you more significant than a friend, they would have been planning our wedding before the birthday cake got cut. They've been waiting for me to find a proper girlfriend for so long that I think they believe it's never going to happen.'

A proper girlfriend? A significant relationship?

'Oh… *Jack*…' A part of Harriet's brain was making a final search to find another way to stop this roller-coaster and keep them both safe from any kind of heartbreak. But he hadn't said that he was in love with her and she hadn't said anything like that either. Surely any relationship had to start somewhere so that you could find out where it might lead? She could actually feel the moment when her brain simply gave up and shut some internal door in her head.

This was happening. Whether this was the real thing or simply physical attraction or gratitude or whatever, she couldn't stop it. She didn't *want* to stop it.

Apparently Jack could feel that door closing as well. Because he was smiling again. Drawing Harriet back into the circle of his arms. Kissing her forehead and then the tip of her nose before his lips settled once again onto hers. And this time there was no soft conversation of questions and answers. They had both willingly climbed instantly onto a new kind of roller-coaster that was purely physical for the moment. A steep climb as increasing desire made this so urgent and a wild descent into bliss as skin was exposed and touched in ways that made intimacy feel completely new.

'Not here...' Jack's voice was raw as he finally held Harriet away from his body.

'I know...' Harriet dragged in a ragged breath. 'They'll be expecting us back at the party.'

But Jack was smiling. 'I didn't mean that... I'm thinking about sand. You know...getting into uncomfortable places. And...protection. It didn't occur to me to put anything in my pocket for the cere-mony.'

Harriet actually blushed. And she was supposed to be the older, wiser one here?

'Nobody's expecting to see us before the big breakfast tomorrow. They think you got tired because of your leg.' Jack brushed her cheek with his fingers. 'You're not, are you? Too tired?'

Harriet took a slow breath. 'I've never been less tired in my life.'

Jack took hold of her hand. 'See that path over there? Through the gardens?'

'Mmm?'

'That leads straight to my bungalow.'

Harriet started taking a step forward but Jack's hold on her hand stopped her. A beat of fear that he might be having second thoughts vanished as she caught the mischievous gleam in his eyes.

'You forgot your sandals.'

CHAPTER SEVEN

'So, HOW WAS IT? Your first day back in ICU?'

'Long...'

Harriet settled back in her armchair, still smiling. She hadn't expected a call from Jack while he was on shift and just the sound of his voice gave her a delicious tingle deep in her belly.

They'd been on the same flight back from Hamilton Island yesterday and Jack had insisted on sharing her taxi to make sure she got home safely. He hadn't left her apartment until many hours later.

Harriet would have sworn that nothing could have been better than the first time she and Jack had made love but, unbelievably, this second time had been so much better. Any shyness or residual doubts about the wisdom of starting this relationship were almost forgotten already. This was an unexpected gift in her life and it would be crazy not to accept it. And maybe it wouldn't last because one of them would come to their senses or hit the wall as far as trust was concerned but, while it was happening, she had no choice but to revel in the joy it was bringing. She was almost drowning in it, to be honest.

'I hope they didn't have you running around too much.'

The note of concern in Jack's voice changed that tingle into a squeezing sensation that seemed to involve her heart. Did men realise how incredibly sexy it was to say something that suggested they really cared about you? Not that she was going to tell him how it made her feel. Or that the happiness she was basking in, thanks to their lovemaking, had definitely done wonders for her energy levels today.

'I think I was given the easiest patient there. A sixty-four-year-old woman with diabetic ketoacidosis. She just needed intensive monitoring while we got her blood sugar levels under control.'

'What caused the DKA?'

'She thinks she got food poisoning. She lives alone and was too sick to even think about taking her insulin. She could have died if her neighbour hadn't got worried about her.'

'Was she conscious?'

'Yes, but I had to do a neurological assessment every hour. Along with measuring her blood glucose level and hydration and keeping a close watch on her ECG. She was getting some atrial arrhythmias.'

'So you were on your feet all day?'

'Pretty much. I'm tired now but it was so good to be back. I'm so happy…'

'I'm happy for you.' She could hear the smile in his voice.

'So, what are you up to?'

'Not much right now and we're due to clock off in twenty minutes or so. We've only had a couple of callouts. Car crash up north a bit and a kid in respiratory arrest from an asthma attack who was more than an hour's drive from the nearest hospital. He'll be in the paediatric ICU now.'

'You got him back? From a respiratory arrest?'

'He didn't arrest until we were en route. It was touch and go. You have to be so careful ventilating someone like that so you don't cause lung damage.'

'Sounds like a tough job.'

'I thought the worst part was that his mum didn't get to the school in time to come with us, but it was probably better that she didn't see how close a call it was. He was properly ventilated mechanically by the time she got to the hospital.'

'Is he going to be okay?'

'They think so.'

'Go you.' Harriet's breath came out in a small sigh. 'You're a hero.'

The chuckle of laughter was soft. 'Hardly. Just doing my job. But it's nice that you think so. What are you up to this evening?'

'Hot bath,' she told him. 'And an early night. My shift starts at six a.m. tomorrow.'

'When's your next day off?'

'Friday. How 'bout you?'

'Also Friday. How good is that?'

'It's very good.'

But the fact that it seemed a rather long time to have to wait to see Jack again was a bit worrying. Was she throwing herself in too deep and too fast to whatever this was? Being a little needy?

'We should plan something.' She kept her tone light. Casual, even. 'If you're not busy, that is.'

'I'll make sure I'm not busy.'

The promise in his voice made her smile again but then she heard the strident beeping over the line that could only be Jack's pager sounding.

'Uh-oh… Have to go.'

For a long minute Harriet simply held her phone in her hand after the abrupt termination of the call. She could imagine Jack and the rest of the crew running out to the helicopter, putting their helmets on and buckling into their harnesses, the way he would have done that day he'd arrived to get her and Eddie off that ledge.

They only got called to serious cases so it was highly likely he was on the way to save another life.

He was a hero all right...

The sun was low enough to make the distant Blue Mountains look even more rugged and beautiful. It was a favourite destination for Jack because it often involved a winching job but this time it sounded as if there was a clear space to land near the mountain bike track where a young man had had a serious tumble. That the job might not be as much of a challenge wasn't what was dimming any adrenaline rush right now, though.

Normally, a late job that meant their shift could run on for even a couple of extra hours wouldn't bother Jack at all. It might mean he'd miss a session at the gym or be late for a family dinner but everybody knew how passionate he was about his job so it didn't matter.

It felt different now. Even though Harriet was tired after her first day back at her old job and he wouldn't have suggested a visit or a date or anything, his time away from work had suddenly become a whole lot more important.

His job wasn't the only thing he was passionate about now.

He couldn't stop thinking about Harriet. This destination of the Blue Mountains was taking him back to that dreadful day when she'd had the accident. He would never forget how it had made him feel to see her lying there with her leg all but crushed by that rock. He almost felt responsible, because he'd seen that she'd been standing too close to the path of that rockfall. He'd shouted a warning, even gone closer to grab her hand and encourage her to run to safety, but she'd tripped on the uneven ground and her hand had pulled away as she'd fallen and his momentum had carried him forward for too many steps. If only he'd been a few seconds earlier. Or had held onto her hand more tightly...

But if he had, life would be very different now, wouldn't it? It could well have been Harriet and Pete's wedding he'd been attending the other day, instead of Blake and Sam's.

And that would have been so wrong. Another memory of the day of that accident was how frustrated he'd felt. Harriet's distress had felt like physical pain for him, too, but there'd been nothing he could do to help, other than offer to take Blake's motorbike back to the city. Pete had been the one who should have been trying to comfort her but all he'd done was sit there and pat her shoulder occasionally and he'd actually looked relieved when she'd asked Sam to go with her in the chopper. What had that been about? It certainly wasn't the kind of concern and care you would want from the person you were planning to spend the rest of your life with.

But she'd been in love with him. She would have stayed in that relationship if he hadn't walked out on her, wouldn't she? Even now, she believed that she was the one who needed to apologise. What the heck was that all about?

'ETA ten minutes.' The pilot's voice cut into his memories and Jack forced himself to focus.

'Can you find out if the patient's still conscious?' The information they had so far was that the bike rider had come off at speed, landed on rocks and was having trouble breathing.

The pilot radioed through for the link to people on the ground.

'He's drowsy,' he reported back to the crew a short time later. 'And confused. Doesn't know where he is or what day it is.'

'Sounds like head as well as chest injuries,' Matt said. 'Let's hope we do have a spot to land and don't need to set up for winching.'

Jack nodded but, as he turned to look out of the window again, his brain was already straying back to Harriet. To winching her off that ledge—the first time he'd ever been that close to her body.

He'd been a hell of lot closer in the last couple of days.

That first kiss had been everything—and more—that he'd ever dreamed it could be. All it had taken was that first touch of her lips beneath his own to make him realise that he'd been kidding himself that he'd got over that crush long ago. That he'd accepted that Harriet Collins was completely out of his league and, even if she hadn't been older and part of a cooler social set, she was so much in love with someone else he would never have stood a chance.

He'd actually been in love with her for the best part of the last two years, hadn't he? That was why he could never find a connection with any other woman that interested him for more than a date or two.

Not that he could tell her any of that. It was way too soon.

She'd had her own doubts about them being together like this and he understood. The age thing, anyway. He knew his family would accept her with open arms and who could resist an invitation to be a part of a huge and supportive family, even if they might drive you crazy sometimes?

Especially someone who had never had that as a child. That was a gift he could provide that meant she would never have to feel lonely again.

No...what really held him back was that part of him still wondered if he was going to be enough for Harriet. If, somewhere in the unforeseeable future, another rejection might be waiting for him? One that would be infinitely worse than a request for a date being dismissed as nothing more than a gesture of friendship.

It wouldn't be the first time either. There'd been a girl he'd been close to, back at university but she'd broken off their relationship when someone more exciting had come along.

'You're such a lovely guy, Jack. I love you to bits...as a friend...'

How could he compete with even the memory of someone who'd been the poster boy for the fire service? The first one to be picked for their famous yearly calendars? He'd seen one of those shots of Pete, with his uniform pants unbuttoned, held up only by suspenders over a bronzed, body-builder's bare chest. He'd been holding a kitten or puppy or something and that sun-streaked blond hair had oozed a beachy surfer vibe. He could imagine how many women had envied Harriet.

'Target sighted, four o'clock,' Matt said.

The helicopter dipped and turned and, this time, Jack managed to push any thoughts of Harriet firmly into the background. Only time would tell if this miraculous new connection would become solid enough to trust that he was enough for her. And he could take it as slowly as he needed to. He'd waited this long so it would be a huge mistake to rush things.

At least he knew he had everything needed to do this job well. And someone was waiting for them who needed their help. And there it was, finally. The adrenaline rush of potentially being about to save a life.

'So he had a flail chest and a haemopneu-mothorax that was starting to tension and we had to get a chest drain in as soon as possible but his head injury was bad enough to be making him really combative.'

'Did you sedate him?' Harriet had stopped eating her lunch, a forkful of salad poised halfway to her mouth.

'He would have been another respiratory arrest to cope with if we hadn't. It was a full-on job, that's for sure. I went for a run when I finally got home, just to unwind.'

'A soak in the bath works wonders for me.' Harriet was eating again. Enjoying this lunch in one of her favourite beach-side cafes. Enjoying being with Jack again after the pressures of their work had separated them for days. 'I've needed a few of those this week.'

'But you've done it. You've managed your first full week back in ICU. How's the leg holding up?'

'Better than I expected.' But Harriet made a face. 'Don't think I'll be running any time soon, though.'

'Never say never.'

'You're right. Six months ago I would never have believed I could walk down the aisle with Sam without a brace, let alone without even limping. Oh…she's sent me through some of the first photos.' She pushed her plate to one side and reached for her phone. 'Some of them are gorgeous. Look…'

That wonderful day on Hamilton Island had been special enough because it had been the wedding of two of their closest friends, but because it now also marked the beginning of what they had between them, it was so much more significant.

Jack stared at one of the images for the longest time. The one that had been taken with the men holding the women in their arms, a breaking wave rolling over their feet. It was *such* a happy photo. Sam had her arms wound around Blake's neck and she was laughing up at him, clearly so much in love. But Harriet also had her arms around Jack's neck, looking up at him, and she must have been laughing as well. None of them were looking at the camera. Blake was smiling down at Sam. And Jack…oh, wow…the way he was looking at her. How could she not have known that what had happened late that night had been inevitable?

'This one,' Jack said, his voice a little hoarse. 'I'm going to keep this one beside my bed.' He winked at Harriet. 'After I crop out the bride and groom.'

He held her gaze a moment longer. Opened his mouth as if he was about to say something else but then paused as if he was changing his mind.

'It was the best day,' he finally said, quietly. 'I'll never forget it.'

Harriet took her phone back to cover a beat of disappointment. Instinct told her that Jack had been about to say something very different. A lot more significant but he'd decided against it.

Because it was too soon? Because neither of them could know if this astonishing feeling of connection was going to last or whether it was just a friendship that had slipped into something more?

'They're due back from their honeymoon tomorrow.' Harriet kept her tone light. 'I hope they've had an amazing time.'

'I'm sure they have. Maybe I'll see Blake at the gym this week and we can shoot a few hoops.' He raised an eyebrow. 'He'll be ready to think about the team again by then. When he knows that you're back on deck in the ICU, I reckon he'll agree it's time you came back on the team properly.'

Harriet caught her breath. 'Do you think? Do you really think I could do it—without risking being a problem for everybody else?'

'I know you can.' Jack reached out and put his hand over hers and squeezed it. 'Look how far you've come already.'

'I know I can walk well. And swim. But I don't think I can run. And I haven't even tried climbing properly.'

'Then let's work on that together. Some walks with a little bit of jogging to start with. Some easy work on the climbing wall at the gym.'

He was back in his very personal trainer mode. Was this the real bond between them? The only bond apart from the intense physical attraction? It wasn't disappointment that ambushed Harriet this time. It was more like…fear.

She swallowed whatever it was. 'Let's do that,' she said. 'Let's start this afternoon. And then…maybe we can go back to my place and…um…have dinner?'

'Oh, we'll have something all right.' Jack's smile told her that food was a very unimportant item on the agenda. He gave her hand another squeeze and then let go, tilting his head to peer under the table. 'You're wearing your trainers. Let's head somewhere nice and see what your leg thinks about a very gentle re-introduction to jogging.'

'I'm up for it.' Harriet slipped her phone—and those photos—back into her bag. 'But don't say anything to Blake yet, okay? Not until I'm sure I'm ready.'

It was nearly a month before Harriet felt she was nearly ready to put her hand up to be on the team again.

A month where she and Jack had been spending more and more of any free time they had together. Time when they were learning that, despite any difference in their ages or backgrounds, they had more in common than they might have believed.

'You like rom coms? No way… I would have guessed action movies for sure. Testosterone and guns.'

'I like them, too. But I grew up with a bunch of sisters, don't forget. I got outvoted every time it was movie night at home.'

Their beach walk that day, with some jogging on firm sand, had become a competition to identify the best romantic movie they had ever seen and the arguments, punctuated by a lot of laughter, had made it so much easier to cope with any pain from pushing herself physically.

Eating together became a real pleasure as they discovered they loved the same kind of food, especially the less healthy treats. Hot, crusty bread with butter and raspberry jam. Fish and chips. Chocolate fudge brownie ice cream.

'We'll have to do twice as much jogging this week, babe...'

And as for the sex...

It took only a look to ignite a desire that seemed to be growing instead of being slaked. Just a touch or maybe a lick to change the pace from a deliciously slow exploration to an urgent need to reach that point of absolute bliss as soon as possible. The time after that was even better, in a very different way, when they could lie together, skin to skin, with their limbs tangled, and they could just breathe and feel the beat of each other's hearts.

That had become the time that Harriet loved the most. The place she would choose above anything else if she needed to feel protected.

Loved.

But while Jack told her in a dozen different ways, through his touch or his thoughtfulness or even simply his smile, how much he cared about her, he'd never actually said the words. Neither had Harriet but it didn't seem to matter. They were together and their bond was getting stronger every day. They hadn't advertised their relationship in any way but it was only a matter of time before others were aware that this was a great deal more than friendship. And maybe it was something that needed to happen slowly so that people got used to it and nobody would say anything that had the potential to dislodge the foundations of what they were building around them.

'What's going on with you two?'

'Huh?' Jack didn't take his eyes off Harriet. She was several metres off the ground and the next hold on the wall was one she needed to access with her left foot. It was a good-sized boulder but this was still going to be a real test of whether she could trust the damaged muscles in her leg to take enough of her weight. She was safe enough, of course. As a certified climbing wall instructor, Jack had tied her into her harness himself, with a figure-eight follow-through knot. He was clipped to a floor anchor and he had control of her ropes as her belayer.

'We're just doing a bit of training,' he added. 'Harry's giving the orange route a go tonight.' He was giving her a little rope with his guide hand as he spoke, his other hand ready to act as the brake in an instant, to limit the distance she could fall if she missed her footing. Or her leg wasn't up to this new challenge.

'I'm not talking about the climbing,' Blake murmured. 'I was watching you when you were getting ready and... I dunno... I got the feeling there's something going on.'

Jack said nothing. He was too focused on what Harriet was doing to respond anyway.

'Keep your arm straight,' he called. 'Find

your centre of gravity and keep it close to the wall. Step with your toes and push off with your leg, don't pull with your arms.' He held his breath for a moment as her foot landed on the boulder and Harriet twisted a little to stay balanced. He could feel his own muscles tightening as he willed her leg to be strong enough to push her upwards and he let out a huff of breath as she succeeded.

He adjusted the ropes he was holding once again. 'Keep going, babe. You're doing great...'

'"*Babe*"...?' He could hear Blake's grin around the word. 'I *knew* it... You and Harry, huh?'

'Yeah...' Jack slid a quick sideways glance at his friend. 'Me and Harry.' His tone was almost a challenge but their relationship couldn't be used as an excuse not to let Harriet back on the team, could it? Not when Blake and Sam had hooked up to the ultimate degree and were both still team members.

Blake shook his head. 'Should've seen

that coming, I guess. What with all the time you two have been spending together lately.' He was still grinning. 'Puts a whole new spin on personal training...'

'That's all it was to start with.' Jack was watching Harriet again as he handled the ropes. She was almost at the top and had to be tired but she was smashing this challenge. The way she had with pretty much every challenge he'd ever seen her take on.

And he was so proud of her he could burst.

'How 'bout that?' he said, as Harriet let out a whoop of triumph on reaching the last set of holds. 'Is she awesome, or what?'

'Amazing,' Blake agreed. He waved at Harriet as she relaxed into her harness, enjoying her success before starting her descent. 'I can't believe how well she's managed to rehabilitate herself.'

'Hey, Jack?' Harriet called. 'I'm ready to come down now.'

He gave her the rope she needed slowly and steadily. 'She's ready for more than this,' he told Blake. 'She's ready to come back on board for the team.'

Harriet landed on the floor and began to unclip herself from the ropes.

'It's lucky you're here to see this,' Jack added as he moved towards her to help. 'Maybe you can invite her back yourself and save her having to ask.'

Blake made a grunting sound but he stayed where he was, watching as Jack helped pack up the gear they'd been using. Then he walked towards them.

'Looking good, Harry,' he said. 'Well done.'

'I know, right?' Harriet was beaming. 'I can't believe I just did that.' Her gaze swerved to Jack and he knew he was smiling just as hard. 'You were right... I *can* do it.'

Jack turned his head and raised an eyebrow at Blake to go with his pointed look.

Blake cleared his throat. 'Reckon it's time we had you back on board for the team,' he said. 'If you want to be.'

Harriet's grin faded until her face was as

serious as Jack had ever seen it. Her eyes were still shining but he suspected it could be from an unshed tear or two. He could feel a bit of lump in his own throat. How amazing was this, to see the person you loved this much achieving a huge milestone towards being the person they most wanted to be?

Harriet didn't say anything, she simply nodded.

'There's a team meeting next Wednesday, then,' he added. 'And make sure you've got your pager with you from now on.' Blake made it sound as if a callout could happen at any moment. Which, of course, it could. 'Jack? You fancy shooting a few hoops before you go?'

'Next time, mate.' Jack looped his arm around Harriet's shoulders. 'We've got a spot of celebrating to do right now.'

It was Blake's turn to raise an eyebrow. 'Sam thinks you guys are just good friends,' he muttered. 'How come she doesn't know about the benefits bit?'

Harriet was smiling again. 'I haven't

seen her for a while. She's too wrapped up in being a new wife, I think. Tell her I'll call her soon.'

Jack picked up the coils of rope and the harnesses and led the way to the equipment room. Was that all this was as far as Harriet was concerned? A friendship... with *benefits*?

Maybe it was time to tell her how he really felt. But what if it was too soon? The seed of doubt was disturbing but undeniable. Harriet hadn't even told her best friend what was going on yet and Jack knew that girls spent an awful lot of time discussing important emotional stuff. Had she not told Sam because it wasn't important enough yet? Because she wasn't sure that what he could offer was as much as Pete had given her?

It was getting harder to close down the urge to push things forward but Jack knew he had to try. This was too important to risk damaging.

CHAPTER EIGHT

LIFE WAS ALMOST back to normal.

But everything felt so very different.

The ache in her leg was so familiar now that it was just a part of day-to-day reality. Soaking it in a fragrant, hot bath at the end of a long day had become one of life's new pleasures.

With a deep sigh, Harriet rested her head against the back of the bathtub and closed her eyes. She needed to make the most of tonight's soak because she wouldn't get one tomorrow with the team meeting being the focus of the evening.

Yes…everything was the same, but different. A year ago she'd thought she'd had everything she wanted in her life. A job she loved, the added excitement of being part of the SDR team, great friends and a relationship that seemed to be heading for forever. But life could change in a heart-beat, couldn't it?

Even now, she could relive that instant in time when her life had been shattered so convincingly. Standing at the bottom of that cliff on a team training day, having completed her abseil some time ago, she was watching Sam take on the challenge. Holding her breath, because she really wanted her friend to ace this and get to achieve her dream of being accepted into the team. She'd actually seen the moment that rockfall had started and she'd been terrified that one of those boulders was going to hit Sam as it bounced down the cliff. And then she'd heard the warning shout and Jack had grabbed her arm and then her hand and he had tried to pull her to safety. She'd tried to run but…she'd tripped, ripping her hand from Jack's grip, and she'd fallen and…

Harriet's eyes snapped open. The jolt of pain that had just flashed from her ankle right up to her back had to be imaginary.

Just a nightmarish flashback. She hadn't thought about the day of the accident with a clarity like this in months. She'd almost forgotten that it had been Jack who'd tried to save her.

She'd never thanked him for that, had she? The time between the rock hitting her and waking up after her surgery was a bit of a blur but she knew she'd been looking for the people that mattered most to be with her. Pete. And Sam. That Jack had now become the most important person in her life was a twist of fate that would have been unimaginable that day.

But it was also one of life's new pleasures.

No…it was way more than that.

The pieces of her life had been put back together. She was coping with her beloved job in the ICU and now had the excitement of knowing that she would be part of the next callout for the SDR team, but her relationship wasn't simply a bonus. It had been Jack's support—his belief in her—that had made it all possible.

She wouldn't be the person she was right now if she didn't have Jack in her life. And she couldn't imagine life without him in it.

He was working on the road tonight but maybe he would call her later, if his crew got a quiet spell between calls. Maybe she would tell him that she'd remembered how he'd tried to save her that day and thank him. Tell him that, while she hadn't had a clue at the time, it was one of the things she loved about him.

Or maybe not…

He had to be the one to say it first, didn't he?

Why? Because that would give her the confidence to take that final leap of faith? To let her get rid of the fear that giving someone that kind of trust was too much of a risk?

Jack would be taking a risk as well. Blake had certainly seemed surprised the other night at the gym when he'd realised that there was more than friendship going on between her and Jack. Did that have something to do with the age difference? He didn't believe it was serious either, or why would he have made that comment about it being a 'friendship with benefits'? Jack hadn't said anything to dismiss that idea and it seemed like they'd both simply pushed it out of sight and out of mind for the rest of the evening, as they'd celebrated her renewed status as a member of Bondi Bayside's SDR team.

It was coming back to haunt her now, though. As much as any memories of the accident did. Was that how Jack saw their relationship? Had he just been a bit carried away by the moment, after that first kiss, when he'd said that the gap in their ages wouldn't matter a damn when they were old and grey?

No. He'd also said that his family would be thrilled to know he had a 'proper' girl-friend, and he'd been right. Only last night they'd been to have dinner with his older sister, Talia, her husband Mark and their three gorgeous small children, who'd cuddled up to their Uncle Jack and accepted their new 'Aunty Harry' without a beat of hesitation.

There'd been a moment when Talia had been busy with something in the kitchen and Mark had gone to get some beers from the fridge in the garage, having handed the youngest of his offspring, Minny—the cutest six-month-old ever—to Jack. Harriet had had to shuffle over to make room for the baby's siblings, who'd crowded onto the small couch to join them and share in the cuddles.

They'd all been laughing as Talia had poked her head through the door to see what the commotion was all about. She'd laughed as well.

'Suits you,' she'd said. And then she'd disappeared into the kitchen again. 'You may as well get used to it, I guess.'

Jack had caught her gaze and he'd wiggled his eyebrows and she had grinned back even though she'd been trying to gently extract some small sticky fingers from her hair.

Of course they both saw kids in their future. It was a question of 'when', not 'if'. And how beautiful would those babies be, with Jack as their father?

But he was only twenty-eight. It could be years before he felt ready for that role. And Harriet was thirty-four, nearly thirty-five. Was that hollow feeling in the pit of her stomach, as she remembered the moment, her biological clock starting to tick? It was probably true that this kind of age gap meant nothing when you were older but they were at a stage of their lives when it could create an issue and put pressure on a relationship.

Harriet sat up and pulled the plug from her bath. The water was getting cool but she had no desire to top it up. To do so would invite tapping even deeper into those insecurities she'd never quite squashed about the wisdom of allowing this relationship to develop. The bottom line was that she would trust Jack with her life.

Maybe she just needed to start trusting him with her heart as well.

'So...you and Jack...' Sam had waited only until Blake and Jack headed to the bar to get their drinks and some snacks before grinning at Harriet. 'When were you going to tell me?'

'We haven't spent any time together since you got back from your honeymoon.'

'I know... I'm sorry. I'm a bad friend. But not as bad as you, keeping a secret like this. I do still have a phone, you know.'

'I know. And I'm sorry. I guess I was waiting to see if it was really going to last.'

'Why wouldn't it? He's obviously crazy about you.' Sam lowered her voice. 'And he's gorgeous.' She cast a glance over her shoulder to check that the men were still in the queue. 'So when did it start?'

'Um...' Harriet almost blushed. 'At your wedding...'

Sam gasped. 'No way…you mean when you disappeared and were worried about your leg and I sent Jack to try and find you?'

'Mmm…' Harriet couldn't help smiling. 'He found me.'

'And I didn't suspect a thing at breakfast the next day. I can't believe you didn't tell me.'

'It felt a bit weird for a while,' Harriet confessed. 'You know…with the age difference.'

'Oh, *pfft…*' Sam made a dismissive movement with her hand. 'If the age gap was the other way around, nobody would blink an eye, would they?'

'I guess not.' Harriet tilted her head to warn Sam that their drinks were on the way.

'Anyway. I'm thrilled. Couldn't happen to two nicer people. I'm so happy for you.'

'Happy about what?' Blake put a glass of wine in front of Sam. Jack was carrying one for Harriet.

'That Harry's back on the team, of

course.' She caught her husband's look and her lips twitched. 'Okay… I'm also happy to have it confirmed that Harry and Jack are an item.' She raised her glass in a toast and then grinned at Blake. 'Are you making an announcement under "new business" at the meeting tonight?'

He laughed. 'Only if Jack and Harry really want me to.'

Jack's gaze caught Harriet's. There was laughter in his eyes but a question as well. About whether she was ready for the whole world to know how they felt about each other. The warmth in this look suggested that he was more than ready and Harriet felt suddenly completely confident. In him. In *them*. In their future.

'Why not?' she said, holding his gaze.

'Ah…because we have actual team business to deal with?' Blake shook his head. 'And I don't want word to get around that the SDR is really a secret dating agency.'

The sound of laughter faded as Harriet dropped her gaze, cringing just a little. Had Blake forgotten about her and Pete?

They'd been an item within a week of him joining the team.

Fortunately, the arrival of their bar snacks diverted everybody.

'We don't have much time,' Blake warned, passing a basket of tiny spring rolls and sa-mosas, along with their dipping sauces. 'I need to be back in twenty minutes to set up for the meeting.'

As usual, it was Blake who was chairing the Specialist Disaster Response team meeting.

The room, not far from the theatre suite at Bondi Bayside, was often used for staff meetings or visiting speakers and it had the benefit of tiered seating and a screen for data projection. It was an easy venue for all the medics involved with the team who were available on any given evening but it was also open to interested people from the emergency services they worked closely with, like the fire service and ambulance.

Harriet and Jack chose seats together

quite high in the room and Sam sat beside Harriet.

'First order of new business,' Blake said after welcoming the group, 'is that we have a potential new member. I'd like to welcome Tim Schofield to the meeting.'

A man in the front row raised his hand and there was a polite round of handclapping.

'Many of you know Tim as one of our best anaesthetists,' Blake continued, 'and he's keen to come to our next training session to see if he's up for the challenge of joining us. Please give him any encouragement because it would be a major asset to have him on board. It would give us a valuable resource for the kind of pre-hospital surgical trauma management that's usually beyond our current scope, especially in an isolated environment.'

Blake was scanning the upper rows now and he smiled as he caught sight of Harriet.

'Next bit of news concerns someone we all know and love,' he said. 'Welcome back, Harry. I know I'm not the only person here who's delighted that you're back up to speed.'

Harriet ducked her head, not having expected the attention. She felt Jack's hand cover hers and give it a squeeze and, for an uncomfortable moment, she wondered if Blake was going to say something about her and Jack once this new round of applause died down.

The clapping was more enthusiastic this time, accompanied by a cheer or two, and every head turned to look up at Harriet.

Which was probably why nobody noticed the door at the front opening. Or that a latecomer was approaching Blake.

'Sorry I'm late, mate,' he said. 'I'm still getting the team emails so I figured I'd still be welcome.'

Blake's mouth opened and then shut.

Sam turned to look at Harriet, her eyes wide with what looked like shock, and, in the same instant, Harriet felt Jack's hand go rigid over hers and then slide free.

'Did you *know*?' Sam whispered. 'That Pete was back?'

'Of course not,' Harriet muttered.

Heads were turning again but the expressions on people's faces were very different from those of a moment ago.

Her ex had just walked back into her life and everybody was curious about what her reaction might be.

Shock. That's what it was.

She sat there, unable to move even her line of sight, which was unfortunate because that was filled by Pete, as he walked towards an empty seat in the front row.

He looked exactly the same as ever. Tall, blond, confident...

What was he doing back in Sydney?

Back at a team meeting?

The joy of having just been welcomed back herself had been hijacked. Had it only been less than an hour ago that she'd felt such a blast of confidence about her relationship with Jack? She could feel how tense he was now. As frozen as she was herself. What was he thinking—that she was comparing him to her previous partner and that he was coming up short?

Tilting her body slightly, she pressed her arm against Jack's and, a heartbeat later, she felt him relax a little. Pete was sitting down now and all that she could see was the back of his head with its spiky, blond streaks. Blake had turned to pick up the remote control for the data projector.

'Knowing that we were going to have Tim here, and that there are some of us who've been absent for a while, I thought that a good topic for our professional development this month was a bit of a revision of the purpose of this team.'

Harriet tried to focus. Blake had known that she was coming back but had he had any idea of Pete's intention to return? Surely not, or he wouldn't have joked about making a public announcement about her and Jack. He would have warned her. They all knew how devastating it had been when Pete had backed away from their relationship in the wake of her accident. When he'd moved out of her apartment. When he'd hooked up with someone new and finally left town.

She might be completely over Pete but echoes of the old feelings were still there. Anxiety. Fear. Rejection. Loneliness. Anger...

Baggage, that's what it was. And she wasn't the only person who was going to have to deal with it. Jack would have his own feelings about it all. Maybe he was thinking about the way his offer of support had been rejected back in those early days after the accident, when all she'd wanted had been for Pete to demonstrate that he'd really cared.

A slide had appeared on the big screen at the front of the room as the lights had dimmed a little. Blake's voice was calm.

'The World Health Organization defines a disaster as an event when "normal conditions of existence are disrupted and the level of suffering exceeds the capacity of the hazard-affected community to respond to it".' Blake clicked his laser pointer. 'An MCI, or Multiple Casualty Incident, is more common and is defined as a situation that places a significant demand on medical resources and personnel.'

He glanced at Tim the anaesthetist. 'Our Specialist Disaster Response team can—and does—respond to both disasters and MCIs, a recent example being the callout to that landslide that buried the ski village. There's a fine line between disasters and MCIs and our objective is always the same. To get the best possible patient outcomes for the greatest number of victims.'

Harriet had heard all about that disaster callout to the landslide from both Sam and Kate, who'd still been her neighbour at the time. More than she'd wanted to hear, in fact, because she'd still been in the mindset of having lost the most important things in her life. Her job, her place on the team. Pete...

The days before she'd reconnected with Jack. Before he'd helped her regain everything that she'd lost. She leaned into him again, and this time his hand slid back to catch hers and her breath escaped in a small, relieved sigh. It was going to be all right. Wasn't it? Every relationship got tested at some point and this situation looked like it was setting itself up to be their test.

She just had to convince Jack that Pete was part of the past. He was unimportant and he couldn't threaten what they had.

'Are you sure you're okay?'

'Of course.' Harriet was kneeling in front of the coffee table in her living room. She'd spread out the handouts Blake had provided at the end of the meeting, along with sample triage tags. She seemed to be comparing the algorithms for two of the major international triage protocols. 'START is easier to remember,' she said. 'Simple Triage and Rapid Treatment. SALT is a bit more complicated, isn't it? Sort and Assess, Lifesaving interventions and Treatment-slash-Transport.'

'They reckon it helps the problem of over-triaging.' Jack sank onto the couch behind Harriet. 'And giving people a higher priority than they should get.' He didn't want to discuss triaging patients. There was a far more important aspect of tonight's meeting that they needed to talk about as far as he was concerned.

'I had a word with Pete when the meeting broke up,' he said carefully. 'He's moved back to Sydney, to his old job with the fire service. He wants to be put back on the active roster for the SDR.'

He saw the way Harriet's shoulders moved as she shrugged. 'I guess it's up to Blake whether that happens.'

'Blake asked me how I thought you'd feel about it. He's not the most popular person in these parts, you know. After the way he treated you.'

'It's history, Jack. I don't care what he does.' Harriet scooped up the coloured tags and turned to hand them to Jack. 'Can you test me on these? I want to make sure I remember this stuff.'

How could she simply dismiss the fact that Pete Thompson had come back as if it meant nothing? Did she not want to talk about it because she knew he wouldn't like what she had to say?

He stared at the tags in his hand as he tried to collect his thoughts and then chose the red one.

'Priority One.' Harriet nodded. 'Immediate attention needed. In the global sorting on arrival at a scene, they're the ones who don't walk or wave when asked to move. They don't move at all.'

She wasn't looking at the handout. Harriet knew this stuff.

'Individual assessment?'

'They're breathing, after any lifesaving interventions that are needed, like opening the airway, controlling major haemorrhage and chest decompression.'

'And what else?'

'Level of consciousness—do they obey commands or make purposeful movements?' Harriet was checking off points on her fingers. 'Do they have a peripheral pulse? Major haemorrhage is controlled and they're not in severe respiratory distress.'

'And if any of those things are negative?'

Harriet's face was grim. 'You have to decide whether they're likely to survive given the current resources. If they are, they keep the red tag. If not, they get a black tag which is "expectant" or no priority.'

Jack nodded. The black tag meant a person was either dead or expected to be dead soon.

Harriet was looking expectant right now, waiting for him to test her knowledge on the yellow tags for delayed treatment or the green ones for people with minor injuries that only needed eventual treatment, but Jack didn't want to play this game any more. The knot in his gut was getting tighter.

He dropped the cards. 'You don't need to do this, Harry. You know it. Talk to me instead.'

'What about?'

'You know what we need to talk about. Pete.'

Her face looked pale, making those gorgeous hazel eyes look huge. 'You don't have to worry about Pete,' she said quietly. 'Yes, it was a shock to see him again like that but it's over, Jack. It was over a long time ago.' She offered him a tentative smile. 'That relationship gets a black tag.'

Harriet was on her knees now, close enough to raise her face for a kiss, and Jack didn't hesitate to lower his head and oblige.

But it felt different somehow. This wasn't a kiss that was about to ignite the kind of passion they had both become accustomed to. He could actually feel a tiny tremble in her lips that told him she was a lot more emotional than she was prepared to admit. She wasn't being entirely honest with him, was she?

He wasn't convinced about the black tag idea for Harriet's relationship with Pete either. She had avoided talking to her ex tonight, other than giving him a cool nod. She hadn't seen the way his gaze had followed her around the room as she'd caught up with other team members and introduced herself to Tim. Maybe she didn't know yet that Pete had decided to come back to Sydney because his relationship with Sharleen had ended. What if lifesaving interventions were attempted, on his part, and the item that had been Harriet and Pete was given a red tag instead? The possibility of survival?

Old insecurities weren't that deeply buried yet. He'd always known he couldn't compete with what Pete had to offer. Not when it came to something like charisma. And Harriet had never told him that she loved him. Not with words, anyway.

Harriet was still looking up at him as their kiss ended. 'You going to stay tonight?'

He wanted to. But what if their lovemaking was tainted by bottled-up insecurities or emotions, like that kiss had just been, and it only made things worse? Jack needed to get his head around this. And he needed for Harriet not to look as if the shock waves hadn't worn off yet. Not to be trembling under his lips. And, more than anything else, he needed honesty from her.

'Are you sure?' he asked softly. 'That Pete's not a problem for you? For us?'

'I'm sure.' Her response was immediate. Too quick? 'Believe me—if I had a choice, I wouldn't even want to *see* him again.'

He was there.

Standing outside the main doors of Bondi Bayside.

Clearly waiting for her.

'Go away, Pete,' Harriet snapped. 'I don't want to see you. I certainly don't want to talk to you.'

'I know. I get that.' But he fell into step with her as she headed for the main gates. 'I just want to say I'm sorry.'

Harriet ignored him and increased her pace. The sooner she got out of the hospital grounds the better. She didn't want to be here. Didn't want to be hearing his voice. Especially not with that note of sincerity in it.

Pete broke the silence as they reached the gates. 'I can't believe how well you're walking, Harry. How great you're *look-*

ing. I was blown away to see that you were back on the team again. You'd never know that you almost lost your leg.'

That did it. She had become attractive to him again because she looked like she had nothing wrong with her any more? Because the trauma of the last, long months could simply be forgotten? Harriet stopped abruptly and rounded on him.

'Yeah…well, I *did* almost lose my leg.' Her voice was low and fierce. 'I almost lost everything that mattered to me.' Her breath came out in an angry huff. 'And I'm talking about my job and the SDR team, here. Not *you*. You couldn't even hang around long enough to find out if I *was* going to be okay.'

Pete took a step back, his face creased as if her words were painful.

'I know. I was a complete bastard. And I'm sorry. That's all I wanted to say. I freaked out, Harry. I couldn't handle it. You know what I'm like with medical stuff. That's why I became a firie and not a paramedic.'

Harriet blinked. Was he trying to compare himself to Jack? Had he heard already that she and Jack were together?

'I do care about you, Harry,' he added, his voice cracking. 'I know I didn't show it enough when we were together and I just want to make it up to you...' Harriet shook her head sharply. She didn't want to think about any of it. Didn't want to hear the emotion in Pete's voice that made him sound so genuine.

She turned away. 'I don't want to talk to you,' she said. 'Go home, Pete. Talk to Sharleen.'

She'd started walking but Pete's voice followed her.

'It's over with Sharleen,' he said, speaking fast. 'That's why I'm back. It was a terrible mistake and...and I was hoping that we could be friends, at least?'

Then he was right beside her again and this time he caught her arm and trying to shake it off didn't work.

'Please...?' He had his hands on both

her arms now and his voice had slowed. 'I miss you, hon...'

He was smiling. Looking right into her eyes. Leaning down towards her in a way she remembered all too well. She knew he was going to try and kiss her and, to her horror, she almost let it happen. Because, for a heartbeat, it felt like she'd stepped back in time. That nothing had happened to change everything.

She jerked her head back, out of reach, just in time. 'Let go of me,' she snapped. 'I've moved on, Pete. I'm with someone else.'

'Who?'

He'd find out soon enough, wouldn't he? 'Not that it's any of your business but it's Jack.'

'Jack?' Pete looked bewildered. 'Jack *Evans*?'

'Yes.'

'But...but he's just a kid. One of the lads...' Pete's breath came out in a huff of laughter. 'You're having me on, aren't you?'

Harriet wrenched herself out of his grip.

'Leave me alone. It's over, Pete. It was over a very long time ago.'

'No...' He was shaking his head. 'It's not over... It'll never last—you and him... He'll find someone his own age...'

Harriet was already moving. Walking away from him so fast she was almost jogging. Trying to escape the kaleidoscope of emotions washing over her. That sincerity in Pete's voice. That moment when he'd almost kissed her. The way he'd tapped into one of her own fears about her relationship with Jack.

She was moving so fast that by the time she crossed the intersection near her apartment block her leg was dragging enough to make her limp.

Her spirits were, too.

She was over Pete Thompson. So why did she feel so churned up now?

Did it mean she did still have feelings for him, even if she didn't want to? She *had* been in love with him, once. He'd been the first person that she'd been willing to commit to spending the rest of her life with.

Did feelings like that ever go away completely? And if they did, did that mean she couldn't trust the way she felt about Jack?

She was very close to tears by the time she fitted her key into her door. All she wanted right now was to hear Jack's voice but he was working. Probably in the sky somewhere in the middle of saving someone's life. Doing the medical stuff that freaked Pete out so much.

And how could she tell him what had just happened or how she was feeling, anyway? It wasn't just that he was seeing Pete as some kind of threat.

Was it because she wasn't yet really sure herself?

Not about whether she wanted to be with Pete or not. She was sure about that.

What she wasn't completely sure about was how Jack felt about her. Whether it was strong enough to crush any potential obstacles—one of which Pete had just reminded her of in no uncertain terms.

'It'll never last...

'He'll find someone his own age...'

CHAPTER NINE

HE COULDN'T JUST stand there, holding his car keys as if he'd forgotten what they were for.

Jack had a job to do. There was an overnight bag on the back seat that his sister, Talia, had hurriedly filled, in case his grandmother was going to be kept in overnight. She'd been the one to call the ambulance when Gran had collapsed. And then she'd called him and his boss had stepped in to cover the rest of his shift so that he could go to his family. He'd collected the bag on his way to the hospital. His mother and another sister were in Emergency with Gran but he hadn't had any update on her condition and he had been doing his best to get there as soon as possible.

But, right now, he was watching Harriet

almost running down the street, leaving Pete Thompson standing almost as still as he was himself.

He'd seen them walking towards the gates as soon as he'd stepped out of his car. Had they planned to meet when Harriet had finished work?

It didn't look like it. If anything, it looked like they were having a row. Not that he was close enough to hear anything but Harriet had looked angry when she'd stopped and turned to speak to him.

The keys had dug into his palm as he'd curled his fist. Did she need help? The only thing that stopped him moving towards them was that Harriet was moving again herself. And then Pete caught up with her. He was holding her. Bending his head as if he was about to kiss her.

He couldn't move a muscle then. There was a bottomless pit where his stomach was supposed to be and it felt like he was falling into it.

Then he saw her jerk back and hope rushed in to fill the pit. She was almost running away from Pete. She hadn't wanted him to kiss her.

Except she had, hadn't she? As he watched Harriet rapidly disappearing along the street, his brain rewound that little scene in his head and, this time, he could see that moment of hesitation. Or feel it. And it felt like history was repeating itself, only with a lot more kick to it. He wasn't just asking her out on a date, he was in a relationship with her. And now Pete Thompson was back in the picture again.

Pete was watching her disappear as well. He had his fingers in his hair, making it even spikier than usual, but then he turned back and started walking towards the gates again. Casually, as if he wasn't at all bothered by the rejection he'd just been subjected to. He had a half-smile on his face as well. As if he was actually pleased about something. Confident, anyway.

A flash of anger broke whatever spell had been holding Jack hostage. He wrenched the car door open, snatched up the bag and then slammed it shut. He heard the locks engage behind him as he pressed the remote, already striding back towards the emergency department. He wasn't about to get caught by any encounter in the car park. He wasn't even going to give Pete—or even Harriet—any more headspace right now.

His family needed him.

The first person he saw when he went into the department was Blake.

'Hey…' Despite the cowboy boots and the ponytail, Blake looked every inch an emergency department specialist. 'I've just found out that it's your grandmother that was brought in earlier. Can I do anything to help?'

'Do you know what's going on?'

'Yeah… I checked. Supraventricular tachycardia. Must have been rapid enough to cut blood flow and make her faint. It's settled now but we're going to keep her in and monitor her. She's been started on some medication and I don't think it's anything to worry about.'

Jack had to swallow the sudden lump in his throat. 'I thought I was going to hear that she'd had an infarct. Or a stroke or something.'

'Go and see her.' Blake smiled. 'And you can stay with her as long as you like. Come and find me when you need a coffee or anything.'

Family members kept arriving, although most of them had to stay in the waiting room because only two people at a time could be with a patient in the observation area, and his mother wasn't about to leave *her* mother's side.

Jack was more than ready for a coffee after a couple of hours of what felt like traffic management. He'd send everybody other than his mother home soon. His grandmother was going to need follow-up to ensure that the new medication was doing its job but this was no longer a crisis.

Blake was due to go off shift but he stayed to have a coffee with Jack and they chose a quiet corner in the cafeteria rather than the department's staffroom.

'You look wrecked.' Blake's smile was sympathetic. 'It's under control, you know. Your gran's not in any danger.'

'I know.' Jack couldn't find a smile, though. He fiddled with the little paper tube of sugar, shaking it into his drink. 'I've got other things on my mind as well.'

'Oh?'

Jack picked up the spoon to stir his coffee. 'I saw Pete Thompson outside when I was coming in.'

'Yeah...' Blake's gaze was cautious. 'He'd been in to see me and pick up a team pager. I couldn't really say no when he's been a member before. And a good one.'

'Wouldn't expect you to.'

'Is it going to be a problem?'

Jack shrugged. 'I don't know. Maybe.'

Blake looked serious now. 'We can't have problems on the team like that. You know how I feel about distractions.'

'Maybe I should stand down for a bit.'

'Wait...*what*? No...if anyone's not going

to be on the team, it'll be Pete. Or possibly Harry, if she finds out that it's too much for her.' He was watching Jack's face. 'It's a lot more than a friendship with benefits between you two, isn't it?'

'For me?' Jack had finally stopped stirring his coffee. 'Yeah…'

'What about Harry?'

'I think it is for her, too.'

'You *think*?'

'We've never really talked about it. I've kept stuff light, you know? She was worried about our age difference and I didn't want to push it. And I wasn't sure that she was completely over Pete. She'd been living with the guy. Probably planning to marry him.'

Maybe he should have pushed things. He should have stayed the night after that meeting. He could have simply held Harriet in his arms. So that she would understand that he would always be there for her.

If she wanted him to be.

Had he made a huge mistake in not telling her how much he loved her? That he couldn't imagine wanting anyone else to share the rest of his life? Waiting for a sign that she would welcome that kind of commitment?

Blake's quiet voice broke the rush of unanswerable questions. 'You don't really think she'd want to go back to *Pete*, do you?' His face twisted with distaste. 'After the way he treated her?'

Jack swallowed a mouthful of his coffee. 'You see it often enough. Women who go back to relationships that everyone else can see are abusive. Or wrong for them, anyway. There are some guys that have that edge, you know? That "bad boy" vibe that women can't seem to resist.' He let his breath out in a sigh. 'D'you know, I actually asked her out on a date once? She thought it was just a friend thing and she spread the word. Invited Pete along, in fact—and that was the night it all started between them.'

Blake's huff of sound was sympathetic. But then he frowned. 'You need to tell her how you feel, mate. Took me a long time to tell Sam how I felt and that was when I found out that she felt the same way about me. The rest, as they say…is history. And if she does feel the same way about you, you won't have to worry about Pete Thompson. Or anyone else.' He raised an eyebrow. 'I don't claim to be an expert on women or anything, but if she's bothered by the age difference, I reckon she's the one who needs the reassurance. To be told that it's not an issue. Call her.'

As if to emphasise his advice, Blake's pager sounded, despite his being off duty now.

Except that Jack's pager sounded at exactly the same time.

Three buzzes. A short silence and then three more.

Blake reached for his phone and his call was answered instantly. 'Mabel? What's happening? Is this a Code One callout?'

He was nodding briskly as he listened. And then he cut the call. His chair scraped on the floor as he leapt to his feet.

'Train versus truck down south,' he told Jack. 'Code One. Let's *go...*'

The scene on the rooftop of Bondi Bayside Hospital was one of controlled chaos. The big doors of the shipping container, well away from the helipad, were hanging open and a group of people were focused on shifting gear and making personal preparations.

Harriet was getting into her red overalls with their reflective strips. She hadn't taken the time to change at her apartment, she'd just grabbed her team backpack and got here as fast as she could. She was to one side of the group, near the perimeter fence, which proved useful because it was difficult to try and balance on her left leg when it came to putting on her steel-capped boots and she could hang onto the fence.

The reminder that her physical abilities were still less than they had been was making her nervous. Was she up to this challenge? The flood of adrenaline she'd experienced when her pager had gone off was still there. She could feel her heart thumping and her senses seemed to be heightened. Against the background noise of a helicopter warming up and instructions being called, she could hear snatches of information being exchanged between team members.

'Sounds big... Semi-trailer truck that failed to stop in time at a level crossing...'

'I heard that the passenger train was pretty full. Could be up to a hundred people involved.'

'Who's going in the first chopper, do you know?'

'Listen up.' That was Blake's voice, carrying clearly in the hubbub. 'We're going to run out of daylight soon after we're on scene. Check the batteries in your headlamps. Put some spare ones in your pocket.'

'Harry?' Sam was hurrying towards her. 'You good to go?'

Harriet straightened from zipping up her second boot. 'Just need a hard hat.'

'Come on, then. You're with me, on the first flight.' Sam led the way to the equipment storage in the container but turned to glance at her friend. 'You okay?'

'Bit nervous. It's been a long time.'

'You'll be fine. Even if you stay in the treatment area, you'll be an asset. You don't have to go climbing over wreckage or anything, just to prove yourself. Grab a hat.'

Harriet stepped into the container. Someone was sorting through the bigger packs of gear at the back but she didn't need to go that far. She reached up to take a helmet from the shelf beside her and then turned to find Pete right in front of her.

For some reason, this was the last thing she'd expected to have to deal with. Again? So soon? She could feel herself glaring at him.

'Hey...thanks, hon.' He reached for the helmet in her hands and she let it drop before his fingers could touch hers. 'Just what I was looking for.'

He was grinning at her, clearly excited to be here.

Harriet didn't return the smile. Something else had just been added to the uncomfortable mix of adrenaline and nerves. Something that felt totally inappropriate to this situation, like…anger? Resentment, anyway. This was so important to her and the last thing she needed was something that had the potential to make it a whole lot harder. She turned back to pick up another helmet. She heard Blake shouting again outside.

'Who's got the airway packs?'

'They're right here.' Sam stooped to pick something up and then vanished. 'I've got them.'

'Just like old times, huh?' Pete seemed to be waiting for Harriet. 'Some things never change.'

Harriet ignored him, turning back. She had forgotten to get some extra batteries for her headlamp. From the corner of her eye she saw Pete vanish through the door and felt a beat of relief.

Another figure appeared at the door.
Blake. 'We seem to be missing the extra
IV gear.'

'I've got it.' The person at the back of the
container turned.

Jack…

The relief Harriet had felt when Pete had
gone evaporated as her nervousness kicked
up a notch. Jack had to have heard the way
Pete had just spoken to her and it wouldn't
be doing anything to dispel the tension that
had been there ever since the night of the
team meeting.

'Thanks, mate.' Blake took the pack and
ducked out of the door. 'You're on the first
run,' he called back. 'It's time to go.'

Harriet caught his gaze. 'I am, too,' she
told him.

His smile gave her an anchor in the swirl
of nerves. 'Come on, then.'

She took a deep breath but held his gaze
for a moment longer because it was giving her something else to hang onto. De-
termination. She wasn't going to let Pete's
presence distract her in any way from this

mission. If anything, she was going to use it as even more motivation to do the best job she possibly could. She wanted Jack to be proud of her. Proud of all that he'd helped her achieve.

He must have sensed the tiny hesitation. 'You worried?'

She nodded. 'A bit. I just hope I can do this. And do it well.'

The expression in Jack's eyes was so intense it made her catch her breath.

'I think you can do whatever you want, Harriet Collins,' he said. 'You just have to decide what it is you really *do* want.'

She followed him to the helicopter, crouching as she went under the spinning rotors.

Sam was on board, she noted. And Blake. A few others but not Pete. He must be going with the next group that the chopper would return for. She buckled herself in and resolved not to even think about him again.

But it was difficult because Jack's words

of encouragement were echoing in her head as they took off.

He hadn't been talking about her dream of being back on the team, had he?

Had he been warning her that she had a choice to make—between him and Pete?

That he would even think she might want to go back to Pete was a problem that threatened to be more of a distraction than the presence of her ex-boyfriend. It meant that Jack had no idea how she really felt about him, didn't it?

And why would he?

She'd never actually told him. Because she'd been waiting for him to say something first. Harriet closed her eyes for a moment. Maybe now he never would...

Circling overhead as they waited for an air rescue helicopter to land first gave everybody on board the big picture of what had happened.

And it *was* big.

They had already seen traffic backed

up for miles in both directions on a rural highway that was now closed.

Now they could see the massive truck and equally big trailer that had caused the accident by failing to stop at a level crossing. It was lying on its side, the driver's cab crushed beyond recognition towards where the last carriages of the train had derailed and were also twisted and overturned. The engine of the train and the first carriage looked intact further down the line but in the middle there were at least two carriages that had taken the brunt of the impact, with the sides closest to the truck ripped out completely or mangled into metal shards.

There were already at least a dozen emergency vehicles on the ground. Police cars, ambulances and fire trucks, all with their beacons flashing. From the air, the red, blue and white lights almost looked festive. Every member of the SDR team, however, knew that the reality was going to be grim.

They carried their gear and headed

straight for the scene command truck. Behind them, their helicopter was already taking off to go and fetch the rest of the team. Another helicopter, from a major television channel, was hovering overhead, preparing to land.

'We've got a treatment area set up,' the scene commander told them. 'The ambos will be glad to see you guys. We've also got people trapped in the carriages and haven't been able to get close enough to assess their condition yet. Head count so far suggests that there's at least six people unaccounted for.'

'Fatalities?' Blake was looking at an area under police supervision that had blanket-covered bodies on the ground.

'Seven.' The scene commander's tone was grim. 'So far.'

'Where do you need us first?'

'In the treatment area. But maybe a couple of you could join the teams working in the wreckage, for when we get access to the people who are trapped?'

Blake nodded. 'Jack? Come with me.

The rest of you, see what you can do to help in the treatment area.'

Ambulance service personnel were overwhelmed by the number of people already needing treatment. One team was fully occupied, intubating someone, and others were amongst a small crowd, many of whom were crying out for help. A man walked towards them, holding a bloodied dressing to his head.

'Please, can someone come? It's my wife. I don't think she's breathing properly. She says it hurts too much...'

'Show me...' Sam followed him instantly.

There was a baby, Harriet noted, lying quietly in the arms of a young woman who was sitting on the ground, just staring into space. Was it too quiet?

They had two doctors, other than Blake, who'd come in this first wave. One headed straight to where the intubation was happening. The other caught Harriet's gaze.

'Let's get some triage happening. We need to clear this area of anyone who doesn't need immediate treatment.'

Harriet paused beside the woman with the baby.

'How old is he?' She crouched beside them, putting her hand inside the baby's blanket, both to feel what his breathing efforts were like and to see if it provoked any kind of response.

'Eight months.'

'Is he normally this quiet?'

The woman shook her head. 'I saw the truck coming,' she told Harriet, her voice breaking. 'I saw it coming but there was nothing I could other than to hold my baby as tight as I could.'

'Where were you?'

'In the first carriage. We didn't get hit. We just got thrown around a bit and then the train stopped with a horrible jerk.'

The baby was moving irritably under Harriet's hand and then it started crying. She was pleased to hear the sound but it wasn't enough.

'He'll need to be checked out, because of his age if nothing else. Stay here for now, okay?' She took a yellow tag from her pocket and slipped the elastic around the baby's arm.

She moved on swiftly. Several people had cuts and bruises but nothing major. A very young-looking ambulance officer was putting a dressing on a laceration. They all needed green tags.

'Take these people to the next tent,' Harriet told her. 'And anyone else who's walking and can talk to you.' She could see someone sitting slumped behind the ambo so she moved on again, dropping to a crouch beside a middle-aged woman.

'Hello, can you hear me? What's your name?'

There was no response. She shook the woman's shoulder gently and felt her tip sideways to crumple to the ground. Immediately, she tilted the woman's head back to make sure her airway was open and checked for breathing.

It was shallow. And rapid.

'I need some help here,' Harriet called.

It was Sam who came and a paramedic.

'Let's get her on a stretcher.' The paramedic nodded. 'Red tag?'

Harriet nodded. And moved on.

How much time was passing was difficult to assess. She knew they'd been here for a while because it was getting dark enough to need her headlamp on. Even after the less seriously injured victims had all been moved to another area, there still seemed to be something urgent to be done every time she turned around. Bleeding that had to be controlled. Broken limbs that needed splinting. Head injuries that had to be carefully and repeatedly assessed to watch for any signs of deterioration.

More of their team was here now, including Angus and Kate. The patient she'd seen being intubated on arrival had been taken away by a flight rescue team for transport to the nearest trauma centre but another seriously injured person had been brought in. Jack was beside the head of the stretcher, using a bag mask to assist breathing.

'Head injury,' he said. 'And there's a tourniquet on his upper right arm.' He turned to head outside again as soon as the doctors took over but he spotted Harriet as she hung a bag of IV fluids on a hook beside the patient she was monitoring.

For a split second their gazes held and there was a question in Jack's eyes. Was she coping? Was she okay?

It only took a nod and the hint of a smile and he was gone again but Harriet was left with the impression that he would have stopped to talk to her if she hadn't given him that reassurance.

That moment was enough to give her a new burst of energy. She had no idea how long she'd been on her feet now with so much swift moving, crouching and getting up again, helping to lift heavy people and racing to find equipment or medication needed, but she *was* okay.

Stable patients, including the baby, were being taken by ambulance crews to the nearest hospitals. A bus had arrived to take people with minor injuries to get a thorough assessment from nearby medical centres. The most seriously injured people were being taken by the air rescue medics to major hospitals that could provide emergency surgery if needed.

Gradually, the treatment area was getting empty. Rescue personnel were being sent to take a break in a tent that had been set up to provide hot drinks and food.

Blake came back, his face pale and weary. Jack was beside him and Harriet had to fight the urge to go to him and put her arms around him. He looked more than a bit shattered. Instead, she filled a polystyrene cup with coffee and added the sugar she knew he liked and took it to him. Sam was doing the same for Blake.

'Two more fatalities,' Blake told them. 'One was still alive when they cut through enough wreckage for us to get to him but...'

He didn't have to say any more. Whoever it was hadn't made it out.

'There's still two people unaccounted for,' Jack added. 'So we're staying on. If some of the team want to get back to town, there's a flight leaving soon. There's no real need for us all to stay now.'

'I'll stay,' Harriet said.

'Me, too.' Sam nodded. She glanced over her shoulder as someone pushed their way to the table with the urns of hot water and supplies for drinks.

'I'm not going anywhere. This is great.'

Harriet was watching Jack's face, concerned about just how bad it had been in that carriage, with the person they hadn't been able to save, so she saw the way his eyes narrowed.

'Having fun, are you, Pete?' His tone was cold.

'Best job I've been on ever, kid,' Pete agreed. 'How 'bout you?'

Jack said nothing, which was hardly surprising. Had Pete really just demeaned him by calling him 'kid'?

'I've been with the firies who are trying to get access to the back of the worst carriage,' Pete added cheerfully. 'We reckon that's where the last of them are.'

Of *them*? Harriet just stared at Pete. Did

he actually see the victims of this disaster as real people? With families and friends who were probably frantic with worry right now and who could be about to be devastated by news of their deaths? Right now, it felt like they were extras, somehow, in the movie that was starring Pete Thompson as a hero. Had he always been this shallow? Had he walked out on her when she'd been scarred and broken because she hadn't matched up to what his leading lady was supposed to look like?

She turned away. Walked away, until she was outside the tent. Sam was following her.

'Unbelievable, isn't he? What did you ever see in him?' She shook her head. 'I'm going to find the toilets. You want to come with me?'

'Don't need to, thanks. I went not long ago.'

What Harriet did need was just a moment to herself. To take a breath and try and figure out how to stop her buttons getting pushed so easily by someone who was no longer part of her life but had left enough damage to be a problem. He was the reason she'd never had the courage to say those words to Jack first, wasn't he? She'd been abandoned once. Rejected because of something that wasn't anything to do with who she was as a person but it had made her feel smaller. Less loveable.

And she wasn't. Jack had loved her.

She gulped in a breath. Was it really in the past?

This wasn't the time to even go there. She wasn't as alone as she needed to be to follow that line of thought. There were still a lot of people moving around out here. A lot of lights flashing and the noise of hydraulic cutting equipment in the background. A photographer who was snapping images of the scene, probably for a newspaper. She hadn't even thought to bring her camera, Harriet realised. Because she was a real part of the team again, not just there with a newly invented role because people felt sorry for her.

She felt, rather than saw, the figure who

arrived beside her. The person who'd helped her get back to this point in her life. Who'd believed in her.

'They're going to call us as soon as they get near anybody else in the wreckage, if they're still alive,' Jack said quietly. 'We're supposed to take a break until then.'

'Was it awful?' Harriet whispered. 'The last one?'

'Yep...'

Someone else came out of the tent and Harriet couldn't help her head turning swiftly. The last thing she wanted was for it to be Pete. She let her breath out in a sigh of relief as she saw that it was Angus, heading back to the treatment area. She should probably go there herself and help tidy up and make sure they were ready if any of the missing people arrived needing help but something kept her still. She could feel the way Jack was looking at her.

'He wants you back, doesn't he?'

'What Pete wants doesn't make any difference.' Of course it didn't. He hadn't been there when it counted, had he? *Jack* had. He'd been there for her right from the start of the hardest part of her life, even though she'd pushed him away. And when she'd let him closer, he'd been there a hundred per cent. A thousand per cent. As invested in her achieving success as she had been.

So loyal. So trustworthy.

'I saw you… Earlier today. Outside the hospital gates.'

Oh, help… Harriet had an instantaneous flashback to that moment when Pete had tried to kiss her. This was way worse than anything Jack had overheard in the equipment container.

'He wanted to apologise, that's all,' she said. 'He knows how badly he treated me.'

Jack snorted. 'And that makes it okay or something?'

Something in his tone gave the impression of an anger that Harriet had never associated with Jack. It scared her.

'I know you've had your doubts about us,' Jack said. 'And I get that this is probably making things a whole lot worse.'

He drained the rest of his coffee from the cup. 'It's up to you whether you believe in me,' he added quietly, 'but, for God's sake, Harry. Believe in *yourself.* You deserve better than Pete bloody Thompson.'

Harriet opened her mouth to tell him that she knew that. To confess that she had been confused by Pete's reappearance in her life because it had been so sudden and it had stirred up old feelings. That she knew it bothered Jack and that the tension between them had frightened her because it felt like there was a new obstacle they both had to deal with and it felt a lot bigger than any difference in their ages and how Jack might feel about starting a family and…the fact that he'd never told her that he loved her.

At the same moment that she drew breath to speak, however, the shrill sound of a whistle cut through all the other sounds outside. And the radio Jack had clipped to his belt crackled into life.

'We've found the last victim. Medics needed, urgently.'

Jack crumpled the polystyrene cup in his hand and dropped it.

And then he walked swiftly away without even a backward glance.

Harriet could only watch him, her chest too tight to allow her to even take a breath.

It felt like she was watching him walk right out of her life.

CHAPTER TEN

BLAKE EMERGED FROM the tent only seconds after Jack had walked away.

He had an extra pack in his hands and he was scanning the scene in front of him.

'Have you seen Sam?'

'She's gone to the toilets.'

He hesitated for just a beat. 'Take this,' he said, then, handing her the pack. 'And come with me. We might need an extra set of hands.'

Harriet shoved her arms through the straps of the pack and jogged a couple of steps to catch up with Blake. Her heart was thumping. She wasn't going to be in the safety of the treatment area now. They were heading into the heart of the mangled wreckage of the train and, sharply illuminated by several powerful floodlights, it looked as intimidating as anything she had ever faced. It was one of the overturned carriages and there was a ladder secured between wheels that led up to the side of the carriage that was now a roof.

Jack was already disappearing into a hole where access had been gained through broken windows. A fire officer reached out with a gloved hand to help Harriet climb the ladder.

'Keep clear of any edges,' he warned. 'Some of them are still sharp.'

Another fire officer was on the top. Another ladder had to be climbed, this time down into the carriage.

There were no floodlights in here. Just the beams of their headlamps.

'Over here,' someone shouted. 'Hurry… I can't stop the bleeding.'

Jack was there first. Harriet saw him crouch and then reach under what looked like the buckled framework of a seat half covering the shape of a body. She let Blake get past her and then the fire officer who'd been in the space moved back, climbing over the seat to where his colleagues were waiting.

'Looks like a femoral bleed,' Jack said. 'I've got as much pressure on as I can.'

Blake was bent over the back of the person. 'Can you hear me?'

Harriet could hear the response. A low groan that became words.

'Yeah…can you get me out of here, mate?'

'That's what we're here for. Are you having any trouble breathing?'

'It hurts…'

'It hurts to breathe?'

'Nah…it's just my leg…where he's pushing on it.'

'Sorry, mate…' Jack's tone was gentle. 'But I have to stop you losing the red stuff.'

'He's caught,' one of the fire officers told them. 'We were cutting the frame of the seat but then he tried to move and that's when the bleeding started. His name's Frank,' he added.

'Foot's still trapped.' Jack had angled his head so that the light was further down than where he had his hands pressed to Frank's thigh.

It looked more than trapped from the glimpse that Harriet caught. His lower leg had been impaled by a thick metal rod and the foot was crushed beyond recognition.

Blake's head turned. 'Hand me the oxygen cylinder and a mask, Harry. And get the IV rollout. I want to get a line in and some pain relief on board for Frank.'

The oxygen and mask were in a side pocket of the pack but then Harriet had to find enough space to open the pack properly and find everything that Blake needed. The wipes and a cannula, a Luer plug and tape. A giving set and bag of fluids and then the ampoules of drugs. She was crouched in a position that was beyond uncomfortable but she still had to move as quickly as possible and make sure she didn't make a single mistake.

Jack asked her to find a tourniquet and dressing pads. The awful groans of their patient subsided as the drugs took effect but Blake wasn't happy.

'Blood pressure's dropping. Harry, come and squeeze this bag, would you? Let's get some fluids in a bit faster. And we need to get him out of here, stat.' He straightened up and moved towards the fire officer in charge of this group who'd been searching the carriage. He kept his voice too low to be overheard by Frank.

'Can you cut him free?'

'It'll take time. We'll have to cut through both ends of that pipe in his leg. Even to get the gear in there safely, we'll have to get rid of the seat on top.'

Jack stood up swiftly and his gaze locked with Blake's. 'Take a look,' he said quietly, 'but I reckon that foot's beyond rescue.'

Harriet sucked in her breath with what sounded like a gasp. They were considering an amputation? *Here?*

Working in a medical field, there were always patients that you could identify with in some way. Maybe they were the same age or they reminded you of a friend or family member. And sometimes they were going through something that you had experienced.

Harriet had never felt quite this connected to a patient before. This could have been her, she realised. If that rock had been bigger. If her lower leg had been trapped and there'd been no way to free her quickly to deal with any other injuries.

Had Jack heard her shocked breath? His gaze caught hers as Blake crouched to peer under the seat and she could read the message as easily as if he'd spoken aloud.

The choice might well be between losing his leg or losing his life…

Blake, as the senior medical officer present, clearly agreed.

'We'll use ketamine anaesthesia,' he told Jack and Harriet. 'And go below the knee as distally as possible.' He turned to the fireman. 'Get a Stokes basket down here so we can get him out. And get a chopper on the way for immediate evacuation.'

'Roger that.'

It was the most dramatic medical intervention Harriet had even been a part of but it was remarkably quick and very smooth, thanks to the calm and confident actions of the two men she was assisting. Harriet's job was to monitor Frank's breathing after he had received the anaesthetic drugs and to assist with a bag mask if necessary. Blake did the surgery with Jack's assistance.

'That's the medial muscles out of the way. Look, the tibia's already broken above where that pipe went through. All we need to do now is cut through the lateral muscles and use the Gigli saw, if we need to, for the fibula.'

Harriet had to close her eyes in the moment the final cut was made.

This could have been her fate so easily. It had been touch and go in the aftermath of her accident and, for a while, she'd had to imagine what life would be like if she'd lost her leg.

But she hadn't.

Not only that, she'd fought her way back to reclaim her life.

Jack had been right, hadn't he? She

shouldn't ever be ashamed of her scars. They were something to be proud of. A symbol of courage and stamina. For the rest of her life, they would be there to remind her of that struggle. And to remind her of the person who'd been by her side every step of the way. She had been very lucky to keep her leg.

But she'd been even luckier that Jack Evans had come into her life.

It was Jack's turn to take the lead now as they got Frank out from the tangle of metal and upholstery and strapped him safely into the Stokes basket so that the team of fire officers could lift him clear of the carriage. Blake was staying as close as possible to their patient, the bag mask in his hand, but Jack wasn't far behind.

Harriet was well behind by the time she got up the ladder and out of the entry access. Her leg had been squashed into awkward positions and now it was threatening to give way on her each time she put her whole weight onto it.

She saw that the stretcher was already

reaching ground level, where a team of people was waiting to rush it to the treatment area. A television crew was nearby, clearly filming the drama. Jack was already on the second ladder but his head was still over the top and he saw Harriet stumble as she stepped towards him.

'You okay?'

Harriet nodded. She couldn't fall at the last hurdle, could she? It would be too disappointing. For Jack as well as herself.

Gritting her teeth, she reached the ladder, knowing that her limp had to be visible. Jack moved down as she turned but she felt his hand reaching for her. Supporting her.

He had his arm right around her as she stepped off the final rung.

'I'm okay,' she told him. 'Honestly… I just need to rest for a moment. You go ahead.'

'I'm not going anywhere without you.'

'But…' Harriet turned to where Frank's stretcher was already at the entrance to the treatment area tent. The television crew was in hot pursuit and others were heading in that direction as well.

'Every doctor on scene will be in there,' Jack said. 'They just need to make sure he's stable for transport and then the air rescue crew will take over. I've done my job.' He was smiling at Harriet. 'And you did yours. You were brilliant. Frank's going to make it, I'm sure of it. And, yeah, I know he's got a hard road ahead of him but we both know it's possible to get there.'

He had both his arms around her now and his head bent so that only she could hear his words.

'I'm *so* proud of you,' he said. She heard him suck in a ragged breath. 'I love you, Harry. I could have told you how much a million times by now but I didn't and I'm sorry I didn't.'

Something fizzed within Harriet and burst into what felt like the emotional version of a fireworks show. Relief? Joy? Or was it just love being unleashed, free of any restraints that doubt could create?

She threw her arms around his neck.

'I love you, too, Jack. I just couldn't tell you until you told me...' Her breath escaped in what sounded like a cross between laughter and a sob. 'How stupid is that? I've stopped myself saying it...oh, about a million times.'

Their helmets knocked together as Jack tried to kiss her. Impatiently he pulled his off and tried again. His mouth was pressed hard against her own and his arms were around her so tightly it was impossible to breathe but Harriet couldn't have cared less. It wasn't, in fact, hard enough or tight enough right now.

She had to gasp for breath when he let her go, though.

And then she was smiling and smiling and couldn't stop. Jack looped his arm over her shoulders and they both started walking towards the treatment area.

'We need to finish this mission,' he said. 'So we can go home.'

'Yes.' Harriet tightened her arm around Jack's waist. 'That's the place I want to be. As long as you're coming with me.'

'Try and stop me, babe.'

Harriet was still smiling. 'No. I'm not going to.'

Jack pulled her to a halt. 'How long will it take, do you think?'

'I don't know. I guess there'll be a debrief and then we'll have to wait for space on the chopper.'

'No...' Jack was grinning as he looked down at her. 'That's not what I meant.'

Oh...the love in that look. The promise...

'What *did* you mean?'

'How long will it take to make up for all those missed opportunities? To say a million times how much we love each other?'

'Oh...' Harriet was drowning in that gaze. 'I think it might take the rest of our lives. Until we're old and grey, anyway...'

Jack nodded slowly. 'That's what I was thinking.' His mouth quirked. 'May as well get on with it, then. I love you, Harriet Collins. I love you, I love you, I love you...'

'I love you, too, Jack.' Laughing, Harriet pulled him forward. The sooner they could get home, the better.

'I think I'm winning.'

'You could be right... Maybe I need a personal trainer to get me up to speed.'

'I think you do... Hope you can find one.'

Harriet's smile hadn't faded. She had found one, all right. The only 'one' she would ever need. Or want.

EPILOGUE

IT WASN'T HAMILTON ISLAND but it *was* a beach wedding.

This was much closer to home and there had been no limit on the number of guests because there were plenty of barbecue stations available and everybody had brought something to share, picnic tables and rugs and chairs and games to keep the children happy. And who knew that so many members of Jack's family had guitars? The music was live and loud and too tempting not to dance to as the party really got going.

Hand in hand, Harriet and Jack were simply wandering, stopping to talk to all their guests, unable to resist a slow dance whenever a romantic enough song started, sometimes just taking a moment to stand together and watch others.

'I hope someone's getting lots of photos. I should have brought my camera.'

'The bride isn't allowed to be the photographer. It would get in the way of this...' Jack bent his head to bestow a lingering kiss on his new wife.

'But look...' Harriet's gaze was misty as she turned back to the group on the grass. 'That's your gran up dancing. With Minny. That's the cutest thing I've ever seen. Minny's only just learned to walk and she's dancing...'

'It's in the blood.' Jack was looking pretty misty-eyed himself. 'You'll see... oh, in about six months, isn't it?'

'You still think we should keep it a secret?'

'Well...it is after the wedding, I guess. It has been just about us so far. But let's not make a big announcement. If it comes up in conversation, we can just slip it in and the news will spread like wildfire.'

Harriet was nodding, but her attention

had been caught by something else. A dog had come running out of the waves, a stick triumphantly clamped between his jaws. Behind him, she could see surfers catching the larger waves and, for a split second, she thought of Pete Thompson.

And it didn't push a single button, other than gratitude maybe.

He'd disappeared from her life almost as suddenly as he'd come back into it—just a few weeks after that callout to the train accident. The surf was so much better in Hawaii, apparently. Good enough to tempt Sharleen to join him even. She spared another fleeting thought to wish them well. Sometimes it took something big to make it obvious that perceived problems weren't really problems at all. To shine a spotlight on what was truly important. She squeezed Jack's hand tightly.

He returned the squeeze, looking down with one eyebrow raised. 'What?'

'I love you,' she whispered. 'That's all.'

'I love you, too.' His smile was mischievous. 'Love you, love you, love you.'

'This isn't a competition, Jack.' But Harriet was laughing.

The dog had reached the first picnic rugs now and that was the moment he chose to shake off the copious amount of sea water still clinging to his thick fur. People ducked for cover amidst shrieks of laughter.

'I'm so sorry.' The dog's owner was apologising profusely to the group on one of the rugs as Jack and Harriet moved closer.

'Don't apologise, Eddie,' Harriet told him. 'Harry's a star. He's allowed to have fun now, along with everyone else.'

Sam was still wiping drops of water from her face. Luc was brushing sand off his trousers and Beth was giggling.

Sam shook her head as she looked up. 'I still can't believe you chose a dog to be your bridesmaid. I could be very offended, you know.'

'Harry was just the ringbearer. We decided to keep things simple.' Harriet stooped to pat the dog. 'Oh…he's lost the flowers from his collar.'

'I took them off,' Eddie said. 'I'm going to keep them in a special place. By that photograph you gave me. That was taken at this beach, wasn't it?'

'It was.' Had that been the day that her new, wonderful life had really begun? When she'd taken that photograph and been aware of the first stirring of an attraction that she now knew was going to last a lifetime?

'There's not many dogs that get to be an important part of a wedding ceremony.'

'We couldn't not invite him.' Harriet leaned closer to Jack. 'He was the one who started it all. If he hadn't done his Lassie act on the cliff that day, Jack and I might never have even seen each other again.'

'And I might have died on that ledge.' Eddie nodded. 'But I should probably take him home soon. Before he makes any more of your guests wet.'

'Too late...' Jack was grinning at the sight of Harry the dog now being cuddled by several small children, including Toby.

'I hope he likes sausages. Looks like he's getting some of the leftovers.'

'Oh, no... I know what happens when he eats too much.' Eddie moved away to rescue his pet.

'There's enough leftovers to feed a small army.' Blake put down the paper plate he was holding. 'I don't think I'm going to be able to move for quite a while.'

'Bit different to where you were posted in Africa, then.'

'You're not wrong, there, mate.' But Blake had caught Sam's gaze. 'It's good to be home again.'

'I thought you were planning to stay longer with MSF,' Harriet said. 'Not that I'm complaining you got back in time for our wedding, mind you. We've got the whole SDR crowd here.' She smiled at Kate and Angus, who were sitting close together, their hands entwined.

'Even Alice.' Kate waved towards her great-aunt, dancing away with a crowd, including Jack's grandma. 'Those ladies have got it going on, haven't they?'

'We had a good reason for cutting it a bit short,' Blake added, and there was something in his tone that instantly caught everyone's attention.

'Oh…' Beth's eyes widened, her hand moving to the impressive bump of her own belly. 'Are you suggesting…?'

'It was supposed to be a secret.' Sam frowned at Blake. 'We didn't want to steal any of Jack and Harry's thunder today.'

Harriet and Jack shared a glance. And a smile.

'It's okay,' Jack murmured. 'We've got a bit more of our own thunder, actually.'

Sam's jaw dropped as her gaze flew to Harriet's. 'No way…you're pregnant, too?'

'Oh, no…' Blake put his hand over his eyes. 'The SDR isn't just going to be known as a dating agency. Now people will reckon we're putting something in the water.'

Laughter followed Harriet and Jack as they moved on a few minutes later.

'I think we need to tell your mum,' she said. 'And your gran.'

'If she ever stops dancing.'

'And Talia, of course,' Harriet added. 'And the rest of your family.'

'*Our* family...'

That stopped Harriet. She had to look around at the happy crowd surrounding them. She'd felt the lack of any relatives she'd had to invite to this special day. The SDR team was the closest thing to a family of her own that she'd had in her life.

Until now...

'It really is, isn't it? I really belong.' She reached up to put her arms around Jack's neck. 'I love you,' she told him. '*So* much...'

'Love you, too.' His smile wasn't mischievous this time. It wobbled around the edges, even, but he wasn't going to let his emotions stop him. 'Love you, love—'

Harriet had her finger against his mouth. 'That was it. A million and one. You can stop now. You win...'

Except she didn't really want him to stop, did she? She lifted her finger, stroking his lip gently as she did so. It felt like *she* was the real winner, anyway.

Jack simply pulled her closer, his lips against hers as he spoke softly.

'Oh, babe… Get used to it. I'm just getting started.'

* * * * *